Winter Quarters

Studies in Austrian Literature, Culture, and Thought

Translation Series

General Editors:

Jorun B. Johns
Richard H. Lawson

Evelyn Grill

Winter Quarters

A Novel

Translated and with an Afterword
by
Jean M. Snook

ARIADNE PRESS
Riverside, California

Ariadne Press would like to express its appreciation to the Bundeskanzleramt - Sektion Kunst, Vienna for assistance in publishing this book.

.KUNST

Translated from the German *Winterquartier. Ein Roman*
Weitra: *publication PN 1* Bibliothek der Provinz, 1993

Cataloging-in-Publication Data

Grill, Evelyn.
    [Winterquartier. English]
    Winter quarters : a novel / Evelyn Grill ; translated by Jean M. Snook.
        p.   cm. -- (Studies in Austrian literature, culture and thought. Translation series)
    ISBN 1-57241-123-6
     I. Snook, Jean M., 1952- II. Title. III. Series

PT2667.R525W5613 2004
833'.914--dc22

2004048137

Cover Design
Art Director: George McGinnis

Copyright ©2004
by Ariadne Press
270 Goins Court
Riverside, CA 92507

All rights reserved.
No part of this publication may be reproduced or transmitted
in any form or by any means without formal permission.
Printed in the United States of America.
ISBN 1-57241-123-6 (paperback original)

His proposal had confused her. She has long since forgotten how to plan. She lets the days come and go. Perhaps it annoyed him that she wasn't able to make up her mind immediately. He probably expected something different from her, the woman who walks with a limp: an open reception, outstretched arms or lowered eyes. Perhaps she has squandered her future yet again by hesitating.

Her fingers tremble as she hems Lotte Spannring's dress. In her excited state she no longer dares to make the stitches that must remain invisible on the fine fabric. Quite unlike herself, she pushes the work carelessly aside, even crumpling it against the sewing machine. Max, she thinks for the first time. Max! There she has a name that could belong to her, that could be linked to her own. At this moment she wishes the man into the room. Come! she says. Now she could give him her answer. She is ready. You, she whispers, and thinks of herself as Mrs. Leimer. Enough of Miss Roswitha.

Soon she can be a married woman, a wife. When her husband takes her arm, her limp will no longer be noticeable. In her conversations with herself, she will no longer speak with herself in the second person. If she is even still inclined to have conversations with herself when she has a husband, she will think and say aloud, I. She will reserve the You for Max.

Roswitha, the alterations tailor, can't complain. Business is good. Sometimes something like pride flashes through her mind, but leaves her as soon as she has to go outside. She has never had self-confidence. She opens the window. She spreads out her arms and breathes deeply and has a black night ahead of her that sends the tears to her eyes. She coughs, she barks, unaccustomed to crying. Then more crumbles out of her, it comes from her stomach and rises up and chokes her and weighs on her and squeezes the water out over her face. When it has passed, and she has wiped the tears from her face, and blown her nose, she sits down at the window. She sits there and feels content with everything.

Her life will take a turn for the better. The so suddenly and unexpectedly proposed marriage has always been her goal and her wish; she never dared admit that to herself before. She never forgets her physical handicap and is aware of her tilted appearance even in her dreams: the jerkiness of her movements has also gone into her face and her body; she is merely a draft, a rough draft. Only her hands, which she lays in each other on her lap, please her; she stretches out the fingers of her right hand, holds the back of her hand before her eyes and imagines her ring finger with a narrow gold ring. She will soon be entitled to a ring, as his wife. She is satisfied with her hands, they are slender and elegant. She will astonish Max with them, with these dainty, slim-fingered hands. Her ring finger will delight him when he slips on the ring; no, she has no need to be ashamed of her hands. Although until now no one has paid any attention to them. Other than Lotte. She had once remarked to Roswitha while she was smoothing the fabric around her hips: Your fingers look like spider legs. As long and as thin as on a daddy-long-legs. They look as if they might break off while you're sewing. Then she had to laugh, and she observed her fingers smoothing the taut fabric over Lotte's stomach and cherished the words as compliments. They made her feel warm. Sometimes in the evenings she allows herself a finger play on a cloth before the mirror. She leaves her own figure, herself, in the darkness. Her white fingers dance over the red cloth that brings them to light and to life. She now lives only in her hands. She places the two times five against the light, lets them hop, wriggle and stretch, and takes pleasure in that for a while. Then she becomes uneasy and anxious, a tension in her breast relaxes, there lie the beautiful ones motionless, and she feels as if her life is over, lethargic, despairing. She rebels, presses her fingers against her cheeks, her cheekbones, her forehead, her nose, against her eyelids, on her lips. She kisses the tips of her fingers. With closed eyes, she kisses each individual one of her delicate fingertips with their round manicured nails, she smacks her lips and licks her tongue over her fingers, the backs of her hands, the balls of her hands, shoves her thumb deep into her mouth until she feels nausea, then holds it illuminated by saliva toward the mirror, is enraptured again by its form, moistness and whiteness, and can't hold back from the frenzy of wanting to become one with her hands; she wants to devour her hands, her fingers. She tests her teeth on the knuckles, tears at the joints until the taste of blood makes her sober. Then she covers the little wounds with small, soft pink Band-Aids.

* * *

The day, a Tuesday, had begun like an ordinary day.

In spite of the sunshine it seemed gray to her; she got out of bed without enthusiasm. In front of her house they had begun to erect scaffolding. Soon they would reach her window. The house was supposed to get a new façade. The municipality was planning jubilee celebrations. The place should make an attractive impression on the expected visitors.

During breakfast she was disturbed by pounding on the outer wall; masons were knocking off the plaster. When she went to the window she saw half a dozen men busying themselves about her house. Later on she went out. She discovered the scaffolding, smelled the dust, and noticed the scabby plaster and the men, whom she wanted to get past quickly. One of them greeted her loudly and bowed, he even swung his cap as if he knew her.

That's how it had begun. Leaning against the walnut-tree, he held a bottle of beer in one hand and swung his cap with the other. The blue overalls, and his face looking as if it were covered with flour from the mortar dust. She murmured a greeting and stumbled on. What did the man want? Why was he greeting her?

At the baker's she was still so beside herself because of the mason that, quite contrary to habit, she bought two poppy-seed crowns instead of one for her afternoon coffee. But by the time she got to the grocer's she had already calmed down and was content with one tomato, fifty grams of sausage and an eighth of a kilogram of butter; she resisted the freshly made curd cheese spread, although the grocer woman persisted in trying to sell it to her.

When she returned, the man was no longer leaning against the walnut-tree. Obviously he had finished his break. Men in blue overalls were bent over slaving away on the poles and boards. One of them had to be her greeter. It gave her a turn to think she might not recognize him again. If he didn't greet her again, she wouldn't be able to think of him any more. She headed for the entrance to the house and used the iron banister to pull herself up the winding stone staircase to the second floor. She put the shopping basket on the kitchen table and unpacked the groceries. For a moment she held her fingers around the tomato, then let it sway on the palm of her hand, spread out her fingers and then coiled them around the fruit again. Finally she put it in the refrigerator. She wished she would meet a sculptor, or that a sculptor would approach her while she was picking up a coffee cup or daintily guiding a sewing needle, acts that she herself sometimes pondered. An artist would, she hoped, be enchanted by her hands, only someone like that would be capable of recognizing the beauty of her hands, he would carve them in stone, he would want to make them immortal. But to her knowledge no sculptor had ever come to her village; and even if one had, how would she, Roswitha, the alterations tailor, have come near him? And how would she make him notice her? Even so, she looked after her hands and finger nails with care.

A shadow fell through the hall window, disappeared again and then darkened the room once more; the shadow startled her when she was standing under the arched kitchen ceiling. She saw poles and boards being lifted and lowered here and there. She went to the window. Just below her, close enough to reach out and touch, two men were positioning a board; two others called from below and waved their arms. One of them could be the greeter, she thought. Then he saw her and called to her: Miss, close the window. It's dusty. She immediately shot the holders out of their lugs and pulled the casements closed. Then she went into the room where she had the sewing machine set up, where she cut out material on the table with the lamp. The window of the sewing room faced southwest. This outer wall was still free of scaffolding. Here she still had an unimpeded view of the parish church with its onion towers, the churchyard and the prison complex. She forced herself to go to the sewing machine and sew a zipper in the postman's pants. The hammering now sounded as if it came from far away. Then she took Lotte's silk dress in her hands and focused her attention entirely on the fine sewing.

Her doorbell rang. At the door stood the mason and asked for a light for his cigarette. Of course she wasn't a smoker, although she sometimes played "smoking" before the mirror with a pencil, to let her hands perform.

She did not invite the man into the apartment, but left the door open while she got what he wanted from the sideboard. In the meantime he had stepped over the threshold without being asked. She was startled by the dirty figure that seemed to fill the small hall. He held out his palm toward her and she put the little box in his hand. He grinned and expressed his thanks with exaggerated bowing. He was gone and left nothing behind but dirt on her linoleum. She wiped the floor right away with a damp cloth and thought, as she did so, that it was always good to have matches in the house.

Now she no longer had the composure to continue sewing the silk dress. It was also time for lunch. After that she sat down again at her work table, sewed a zipper in her brother-in-law's pants and still did not dare to tackle the silk dress, since she feared she would not be able to summon the necessary calm and concentration for the expensive piece. She could still hear the muffled banging and pounding of the men on the east side.

Around three o'clock in the afternoon her bell rang again. At the door stood the familiar worker. He asked if she had time for him for a few minutes. She was so surprised she couldn't answer. Then the man wiped his forehead as if he had to recall something he had almost forgotten. Miss, allow me, he continued, my name is Leimer, Max. She was uncertain what to say to that, drew back a step and murmured: Pleasure.

He followed her quickly and said he hoped she wouldn't be frightened. He had liked her from the first moment he saw her. He had thought to himself that they were both alone, and that wasn't good. So he had been wondering if it wouldn't be better if they got together. That is to say, he was looking for a woman and meant it in all seriousness.

She sized him up. The person, encrusted with dirt, bristly gray hair over his forehead, seemed threatening to her in spite of his smile. His confession seemed to her like an attack. His powerful figure seemed to want to take possession of her and the air around her. She wished him out of the room as fast as possible. How did he even come to descend on her unannounced with such an offer? She didn't know him. Finally she had to rub her eyes: Was she even awake?

He declared again that he meant it sincerely. She answered quickly that she would have to think about it.

Agreed, said the intruder, by when?

By tomorrow, she said, to her own surprise.

By tomorrow then. Max Leimer seemed satisfied with that. He put his workman's cap back on and went. His broad sturdy back, the last thing she saw, was both touching and foolish. She heard his steps on the stairs, and her fear of him faded. From behind, he had looked defenseless. Or good-natured. She trusted his back. Yes I will, she laughed, I'll marry him! Just the thought of getting married! She shook her head: A strange fellow.

She shut the door and discovered his dirty footprints sticking to her mottled brown flooring for the second time today. For the second time she wiped them off.

Meanwhile the sounds of work on the outer wall had ceased. She didn't dare to open the window, because she didn't know if the workmen had already finished work for the day.

In the kitchen she drank her afternoon coffee and devoured both poppy seed crowns. After that she felt sick. That was not surprising, after so much excitement and so much dessert. She lay on the couch and shut her eyes, but needles, thread, measuring tapes, scissors, silk clothes and the mason still kept dancing in her head.

* * *

Tonight she lies awake a long time. Imagining that soon she won't be alone anymore is like having streams of light from fireworks flash around in her head. The crowning touch is a full moon whose cold white light is staring through the curtains, making bizarre monsters of her sewing machine and the articles of clothing piled up for alteration. She sleeps in her workshop, although she has a bedroom. Her parents' marriage-beds are still there. The bedroom is the best positioned room in the apartment, facing southeast, with a view of coniferous forests and rolling hills, she reflects. The river flows past outside. With Max Leimer she would move into that bedroom. In her excitement she slips out of bed, shivering on the smooth linoleum. She opens the door to the corridor that leads to the lavatory and to the bedroom. She seldom enters the room, and then only to let in some fresh air. Perhaps they will need new mattresses? At any rate she has to dust, and polish the brass bars of the beds, and shine the mirror and the glass tops on the night tables. The carpets, which are lying rolled up, should be beaten. She thinks of all that as she feels her way on bare feet along the corridor to the bedroom. She doesn't need to turn on a light. Milky moonlight penetrates the bare windowpanes, shining on the sheet that covers the mirror, and on the wide bed. Its yellowish brass bars shimmer with a silvery luster. She quickly opens both sides of the window. The moonlight is swimming on the river as well, with almost blinding brilliance. The fresh night air smells of fish and faintly of sewage.

She cannot imagine her parents in the beds. She never saw them lying in them. The bedroom had always been tidy and didn't seem lived in even when they were alive. She leaves the window open, patters over to the covered mirror on her tiptoes, puts her feet flat on the floor; she shivers. Her footprints would be visible tomorrow in the layer of dust. There is much to do here; she will begin the work early in the morning. She sneaks back. Specks of dust stick to the soles of her feet. So now she has to wash her feet. She mixes hot and cold water in a wash-basin, sits on a stool and puts her feet in the lukewarm water. It occurs to her that she has never before washed her feet at midnight. She fishes for a towel that hangs on the side of the sink and puts her feet on the soft terry toweling. Her foot with the shorter leg is narrow and bluish; it lies in her hands as if it were boneless. The skin on the sole is thin and smooth like tissue paper, except for a yellow callus on the ball of the foot. With this foot she just treads on the tips of her toes, when she walks it pokes at the ground like a beak, and her body tilts over it. Her stunted leg only reaches as far as her ankle on her healthy leg. No amount of stretching can compensate for that.

When her parents were still alive she had to wear orthopedic shoes. One of the shoes had to make up the missing length of her stunted leg with a high, block-like sole. This shoe made her the laughing-stock of the class. Someone had discovered that her block shoe looked like a coffin. Since then, as a child, she had always had to think of her shoe, that was dark black, as the coffin shoe. Only after her father and mother were dead had she been able to rid herself of her "coffin shoe" and, for the first time conspicuously limping, had taken Martha's arm as they followed their parents' coffins to the cemetery.

When she is finally back in bed again, she thinks of her sister. She must tell Martha first thing tomorrow about her marriage intentions. The thought of it satisfies her. At last she has an accomplishment to announce, something no one would have thought her capable of.

She always wakes up at the same time. Right away, she hears a scraping on the outer wall. The noise from the construction work, that already disturbed the quiet of her breakfast yesterday, bothers her today the moment she opens her eyes. She hangs her legs over the edge of the bed and remembers yesterday. She didn't arrange a time with Leimer. When would he come again? Maybe even in the morning? Or would he wait to see if she left the house? Or approach her on the street? It was stupid of her to have left everything undecided. Now she is at the mercy of pure chance.

Then there is still Lotte's silk dress that she has promised for this morning, she reminds herself. It would be picked up.

Outside they hammer and bang. She is still in her nightgown and imagines that below her window her bridegroom – the word makes her head spin – is standing looking up, waiting for a sign.

She warms water on the hotplate in the kitchen, pulls out the washstand from under the table, puts the washbasin on the stand, lays out the soap bowl and washcloth in readiness and puts the towel within reach. This takes her no time at all. She slips out of her nightgown and bends her upper body over the bowl, dips her lower arms and elbows into the water, begins to rub them with a washcloth, then forms a lather and with her hands cupped shovels the water over her chest and upper arms. Shivering, she reaches for the towel. The floor has got wet. She mops up the puddles and at the same time wipes the whole kitchen floor clean. Again she heats water, for filtering her coffee, which she enjoys with bread and jam.

Later she also opens the second side of the window in her workshop. She sees the nave and towers of the church, the prison wing, and on the lawn, boards and iron bars, tools and buckets, bushelbaskets too that weren't there yesterday. Now two workmen come around the corner, two of the ones who have been working on the front of her house since yesterday. Obviously they want to put scaffolding all around the house and improve its appearance on all sides; not just the front should look respectable. The scaffolding would go up on the side of her sewing room as well, up over the window, and the dust would penetrate through all the cracks, and the men would clamber about before her eyes and apply the stucco, after they had first knocked off the old plaster down to the bricks with much scraping and knocking. That worries her, so she tells herself to cheer up, but still cannot rid herself of a feeling of distress, as if something strange were breathing down her neck; although soon, that must not be forgotten, she would no longer be defenseless here. Max Leimer would be able to leave through the window and he would already be at his place of work. That's hilarious. And their wedding? That would take place in due time. We have to publish the banns, she thinks, and both our names will stare the observant villagers in the face for three weeks, people will think it over and speculate, and perhaps they will find objections to my bridegroom ... In the meantime the work of putting up the scaffolding around the house will continue.

Now her workshop window is wide open, she has fastened the sides of the window properly in place. But that doesn't suit her either; it worries her, because she no longer dares to shut it. The sides of the window clatter and squeak, and if she handled the window she would startle the workers working below or at least cause them to hear something and look up. Perhaps they know about Leimer's proposal and are waiting to get a glimpse of her, to find fault with her or smile pityingly at her. She could be sure of their mockery if she leaned out the window and showed herself from an unflattering angle. If she held her face down with her straggly hair she would look like an old woman and would repulse those below.

    She should be on the way already; but Lotte's dress is not yet finished. Roswitha's hair is still hanging loosely around her shoulders. Individual strands slap against her face. She has to seat herself at the table to work on the silk dress, although she now feels exposed there, too, by the open window. The scaffolding would soon be higher than her shoulders. The brown crêpe de Chine with the little golden straw flowers glides over the backs of her hands, through her fingers, slips away from them, resists their control. The insubordinate silk in her nervous fingers, the trembling needle missing the spot, a prick in her left index finger, drops of blood ... Again she is afraid. So here she sits at the open window wishing it were shut. It's enough to drive her up the wall: In the hall, where she would like to be if the window were open, it is shut. Yet as long as she has to assume there are workers all around the house, she doesn't dare handle the sides of the windows. This is how she imagines she would feel under siege: besiegers coming closer and closer grab at her and will force her yet to jump out the window; that is the only option that remains for her, because she no longer dares to escape into the open through the main entrance. But if she went out through the window, came from above, fell down heavily on the besiegers – that would put an end to everything...

    She stands up and goes to work on her unstylish hair that hangs about her face. This has to be changed. Every man places value on having a well-groomed wife. Most men like curls. Again her appearance in the mirror gives her a start: What a sight I am! She tames the strands of hair, pulls them back from her face and winds them into a bun, holding it in place at her neck with hairpins. The result worries her. Leimer's proposal is a foolish prank. She presses her hands to her temples, folding her fingers over her forehead. At last the mirror shows her her perfect hands. She stretches her arms toward the glass, her form becomes indistinct. In this way she escapes from her meager face. It fades away. Her outstretched, supple white fingers, slender as gazelles, conjure up a delicate face with a smooth forehead and heart-shaped lips on the mirroring surface. Her own physiognomy with the wrinkled forehead and tilted nose has finally gone away.

These hands would indeed be able to grip tightly and hold fast the good fortune that was now obviously coming her way; and these hands would also continue to carry out their work to everyone's complete satisfaction. How had she so easily lost her confidence, so quickly let herself be down in the depths? She sits down at the table again to work on the silk dress and is only initially distracted by the hammering outside; the men's voices seem far away now. Her work goes quickly again, the silk hugs the backs of her hands and complies with her; the stitches succeed invisibly as required. Between the stitches, over the crêpe de Chine, she lets her dreams take her where they will; the work proceeds along with her plans; she dreams she is sewing her wedding dress. A dress of silk. That's how the hem gets finished. Then she irons the dress, holds it up in front of herself with outstretched arms, shakes it and admires the perfect hang of the jabot. Would such a pattern suit her? Something undulating like that under her chin? How would she see herself in that?

She puts the dress on a hanger and hangs it on one of the hooks beside the door, where the finished garments have their place. Now she doesn't want to delay going shopping any longer. She doesn't want to think of Max Leimer again until he is standing in front of her. When she thinks of her nighttime trip into the bedroom, even that embarrasses her now.

She leaves the apartment and goes jerkily down the steps; the front door is open. Bright light lies before the exit like a friendly carpet, on which she steps firmly with her healthy foot, and pokes at it with the other. She sees the construction equipment in front of the house, the piles of sand and bags of cement. There are no workmen on the scaffolding.

When she returns, there is still no one in the workplace. It's possible that everything is being done on the side where her sewing room is, where the window is still open. She hurries into the apartment and runs into the room. Indeed there is banging and dragging to be heard here, sometimes shouting too. But they haven't reached the window yet. She hobbles over. Below her the thick boards are already within reach. On either side of her window, vertical iron ladder-like supports reach up under the roof.

Two men are bent over slaving away at the lowest layer of boards. Others are piling more boards on the lawn that has already been ground up by the trucks and construction machinery. As she cautiously pulls the sides of the window shut, the men look up; immediately, she recognizes Max. He greets her. She thinks right away of her hairdo; one of the strands has come loose again and is shading her cheek, probably like an incision. She quickly pushes her hair back, and in doing so lets go of the window fastenings that swing with a squeaking sound. She tries to smile. Leimer is still nodding and waving when she has already shut the window but remains standing behind it.

Now she opens the window in the hall. She also flings the kitchen door wide open to let fresh air into the arched ceiling. Only then does she hastily put away the groceries she has bought, in the refrigerator and the cupboard. Lotte can come any minute now.

Finally Lotte – ringing impetuously – is standing at the door. She has little time today, she moans as soon as she comes in. I hope you have everything finished. Roswitha, nevertheless, offers her a cup of coffee or a little glass of wine. Lotte glances restlessly at the clock, she is glowing with expectation. Roswitha wants to draw her into a conversation so that afterwards, when she has finished what she has to say, Roswitha can also have a chance to tell her story. No time, no time! exclaims her friend. Oh come on, says Roswitha, and quickly brings out the wine and glasses, Lotte waves them away with her hands, does sit down though and runs her hands time after time over her elaborate hairdo that resembles a snail-shell made of rolled red hair. Roswitha admires and envies her. She always has something to tell. The two friends clink glasses; to your news, says Roswitha and thinks of her own. She has an important appointment afterwards, answers Lotte. Roswitha brings the silk dress. While Lotte is getting changed behind the screen, she learns that her friend has had a phone call from school inspector Hingerl. I'll have to have a telephone installed for me too, thinks Roswitha. Just imagine, says Lotte, he has written an historical tragedy for the thousand year jubilee of the town, and he wants to have it performed in the parish hall. That's nothing compared to my news, thinks Roswitha. The parish priest already knows about the plan and is in agreement with it, calls the voice behind the folding screen. He will have collections taken on the following Sundays to support the project. The mayor is enthusiastic about the idea as well and has promised financial support. Roswitha hasn't paid proper attention because her thoughts are on her own affair, about which she will absolutely have to tell her friend afterwards. Lotte emerges from behind the screen, spreads out her arms: Finally something to do! Roswitha does not understand what she means. Lotte shows her the back, and Roswitha buttons it shut. She squeezes twelve little buttons through the button holes. He says I am the right one, Lotte begins again, goes over to the mirror, raises and lowers her arms slowly, bends at the waist, clasps her hands in her towering hairdo and smiles at herself. Roswitha steps behind her friend, pulls at a sleeve and smoothes the dress over her shoulders and hips. She is smiling too and thinking about Max. Her fingers shine white and slim on the brown silk. I always did have a talent for acting, remember? asks Lotte. Roswitha places her hands on Lotte's waist. In the mirror she sees her fingers lying around the middle like a delicate belt buckle. Oh yes! she says and has to clear her throat. You were the star in our school plays. Lotte turns around, embraces her and whispers: He says I'm a born actress! Who? asks Roswitha distractedly. The school inspector of course; he remembered her performances in school, although he was still a very young teacher at the time. He called her entrances unforgettable! Finally Roswitha understands. Lotte is supposed to play a role in Hingerl's historical tragedy. The lead role, she affirms. What does your husband say about it? asks Roswitha – she is still hoping for a way of moving on to the next subject. Hermann, answers Lotte and looks at herself dreamily in the mirror, is on night duty today. Are you now satisfied with the dress? asks Roswitha. Yes, it fits. Only the color! The brown is really boring. Next time she'll wear everything in red.

Now it's Roswitha's turn. It is essential for her now to tell about Max Leimer. Lotte wants to know how much she owes her. She protests that the payment is not urgent. Just imagine, she begins. No, no, Lotte insists, she doesn't want to have an outstanding debt. So how much? Roswitha quickly names a sum.

She begins again: Today, just imagine ... Lotte lays down the money; it is more than the tailor has asked for. Yesterday all of a sudden, she stutters. Lotte packs her bag. I'll pick up the dress later. Then I'll tell you how things went. She is already at the door, calling back over her shoulder: Cross your fingers for me! A red silk shawl Roswitha has never seen on her before flutters over her back as she runs down the stairs.

She still has Lotte's face, always full of color and freshness, before her when she has to go past the mirror. She ducks. She doesn't want to see her own face now. Perhaps she could learn a little from her friend: a little red on the cheeks and some lipstick would make her prettier too. Lotte's hands, though, she smiles as she thinks of it, are podgy. The short, fat fingers repulse her. Lotte usually waves her arms about, so that her hands are lost in the surging of the wide sleeves and frills.

She hears hammering again. It's almost noon, high time to prepare her meal. She is tired, and would gladly have rested a little now. It's cool in the kitchen, which always reminds her of a cave. It has been familiar to her since her childhood. Her mother sometimes longed for more light and air when she was cooking, when the roast smelled or she was roasting the onions or putting the icing on the Christmas baking. It had always been very pleasant for her as a child in this dimness filled with heavy smells. She liked to sit there on a stool at her mother's feet. In the past, four of us sat around the table that stands with its long side against the wall, she remembers, the place is so narrow between the sideboard and the wall. As if we were tied in a bundle, that's how we might have appeared from a distance as we sat at our dinner-table. Our four-headed bending over the table. Our shoulders bumping together. That's how we learned to eat our soup considerately and carefully. A sudden reach for a knife would have jostled someone else, spilled the soup of the person sitting beside me and perhaps even pushed the person at the end off his or her chair. We ate our meals in silence. If we told something in even a few sentences a spontaneous gesture would have disturbed the order at the table.

He has just left. The door handle must still be warm from his hand. He held on to it for a good while. Suddenly something else occurred to him, when he already had one foot almost out the door. And he stayed standing on the threshold and rubbed the handle warm with the ball of his thumb. But he would soon be here again. In an hour at the latest. Is that the way she wanted it? Was that what she wanted? Or had she been made to want what he wanted? By him? Or by her fear, her inability to say no? She should have asked for another day's time to think it over. At any rate, he explained everything to her; he wanted, indeed had to move in with her this very day, and she agreed, said yes, although he was still a stranger to her and became even more of a stranger during the sentences they spoke with one another, sentences she can no longer remember verbatim. Nevertheless, he obviously convinced her – or only made her feel intoxicated? Will she now become sober again? No, she would have to consider herself merciless if she did not let someone like him – and since she has, after all, decided in principle to marry him – live with her, if she let him go to the dogs out there in the shack where there were vermin and it was generally miserable.

As long as he was standing before her, everything made sense to her. Everything was clear. But hardly had he shut the door behind him and wiped the dirt off his shoes again on her linoleum, and hardly had she had to bend over again to wipe it up when she became uncertain and would rather have slept on it one more time...

Now she has to get the bed ready for him in a hurry. She is determined to let him sleep alone at first in the bedroom. Only when she is a married woman will she lie by his side. Until then she will regard him as her lodger. This thought reassures her to some extent. She has found a provisional form for their living together. In the bedroom she removes the white sheets from the furniture and the beds. She stacks the pillows and quilts on the window sill. And all in great haste. She also washes the floor, unrolls the carpets that should actually be beaten; but there is no time for that now. Maybe Max will do it sometime. She avoids the three-piece mirror, but it surrounds her. It disturbs her that she sees herself across from the mirror and cannot elude it because its three pieces follow her everywhere, showing her from behind and in front, now from the right side and now from the left side when she looks up even a bit from the floor and the cleaning cloth. She has always avoided seeing her hands, legs and head as a whole that represents her. She only ever has individual body parts in view. But this mirror destroys her split way of looking at herself. Suddenly she sees herself opposite her complete figure. Her mirror image burns through her hopes and fears. And everything is in flames. Call the fire department, she thinks. I'm funny. And she stretches out her always beautiful hands in front of her and conjures up their mirror image. It's true that her hands stretch out toward the glass, move like a vanguard before her body, but it still exists in its stunted state, and her hands with their beauty and the slenderness of their nimble fingers, the manicured nails, are powerless against her bent body that pushes itself to the fore, helpless, too, against her face with its pointed nose and the drooping corners of her mouth: While preparing the nuptial chamber, this word actually does occur to her at the moment – she must have read it once – the nuptial chamber, yes, it is found in a fairytale, her nuptial chamber, she, the bride, withers into a scarecrow. She laughs and laughs. That doesn't make her happy. She stoops over her cleaning cloth, kneels down on the smooth waxed floorboards, polishes them, sliding along with her hands and knees on the cloth, her gaze always fixed on the boards, the rag, her hands. Then she gets up, her knees hurt, she limps to the window, shakes out her dusting cloth outside, avoiding the mirror. Again she hopes. It wouldn't necessarily have to be a sculptor. Perhaps a mason would also appreciate her perfect hands. She opens the wardrobe. She looks at the old coats like yellowed photographs of people who have passed away. She gets cardboard boxes and clears out one compartment of the three-part cupboard for him, for Max. Her father's suits appear, bringing to mind the occasions on which he wore them: the wedding and funeral suit, the workday suit, and finally the suit he wore for Sunday walks, it is brown. She also holds her mother's dress for special occasions in her hands. It is made of dark blue woolen cloth. Finally she finds her red coat with the white rabbit fur collar that she had as a girl. She was a seventeen-year-old when she wore that. Dreadful unhappiness rises up from it: the fatigue of puberty and aversion to life; not wanting to be there anymore. The box has gotten heavy. She drags it into the corridor and pushes it under a rack. Then she wipes the compartments of the wardrobe clean.

The pillows and the quilt are certainly no longer the best. In the quilt the feathers have gone lumpy, the mattress is mushy; maybe it would cause nightmares. She will remedy these shortcomings quickly. Maybe even tomorrow. But tomorrow frightens her. She takes the pillow and duvet from the window and puts flowered slipcovers on them, places them neatly on one half of the parental marriage-bed and smoothes them down. Again it occurs to her that tomorrow her changed circumstances would be visible to everyone, namely that she, Roswitha, the cripple, had taken in a man. What would Lotte say about it? If only she had been able to get a word in edgewise, she would have been able to tell her! She feels uneasy; but she tells herself that nothing more can be changed now and that the new life has to be tried and she has to cope with it. At least some excitement has come into her daily routine. She feels the urge to laugh, a whirl of agitation, she sweats. It serves her right.

When her anticipation was at its peak, Max appeared at the door. She took it as a good sign. She had been waiting for him for the past half hour, rigid with tension. She had been unable to leave the armchair in the sewing room. The sounds of work on the outer wall had ceased, she heard voices, the workers dispersing. Now it would be decided whether he would come. She was shocked at her obsessive waiting. What was she waiting for? Did she know what she was waiting for? Whether she was waiting for the man, Max Leimer, or whether it was the change, the newness, that aroused her so. That could not be clarified now. She stared at the door that would soon have to open, the bell would ring, she would call out Come in ...; but she no longer thought that someone would come in, that he would. Nothing mattered now but the ring of the bell, a knock, the creaking of the door when it opened. When she thought she could no longer stand the suspense, the doorbell buzzed; she leapt up, hobbled over, tried hurriedly to calm herself before the still shut door. Then Max had already flung open the door and stood before her. Immediately she shed her fears, perhaps because she had almost run into the open door. He was really there. Actually he shouldn't have been allowed to come. After such moments that almost tore the soul into pieces, or whatever it was they did, there could be no fulfillment. Only a disappointment would have been appropriate. Dirty and smiling he stood before her. His lips, gray with dust, were pulling back over black tooth stumps, he indicated a bow. So that was what she had waited for. And was that now after all the disappointment?

Roswitha asked him to come in. Her voice was still a little breathless, but she soon had it under control again. Where did her sudden sense of certainty come from? I am the warden, she thought. I have the roof, the bed. I am the owner. I can give or refuse. That sounded in her words and made them smooth. He came in, and she immediately thought of the dirty footprints that he would leave on her linoleum again. Now for the third time! Suddenly she perceived that through him many other new inconveniences could also obtrude on her life. And she felt a faint rage against the soles of his shoes. She led Max into the sewing room, where she had cleared aside her needle, scissors and thread, and let him sit down. He looked around. First he has to get oriented, she thought, my workshop impresses him. They were silent. Roswitha felt the silence become uncomfortable. Something had to be said. She began to talk about the weather, and at the same time he made a few awkward remarks to her about his views on Indian summer; both of them laughed as they finished the first sentence in an involuntary canon. Then one word followed quickly on another. Roswitha said she wanted to give him a try and made him acquainted with her workshop. And by and by the whole apartment, and herself. He told about himself and the shack where he had to live. Roswitha went into the bedroom with him following along behind always talking of himself, of his need for winter quarters, and she of the apartment, so that her head was spinning and she remembered nothing more about him than shack and not guilty and set up and slut. Finally they stood beside the bed. Then both were silent, Roswitha was smiling proudly and Max was panting. Then I can stay right now, he said at last and grinned. It didn't do Roswitha any good to talk of tidying and cleaning. In response to her protests, which were probably not forceful enough, he only said "Oh go on, go on." In this manner he invalidated her objections, and finally she had consented and didn't know how. Then he held out his hand to her. She had certainly expected more from the handshake. The rough and chapped palm of his hand lay on her fine, narrow palm. Never had she felt her hand to be so delicate and fragile. Did he feel that? Did he feel what was special about her hands? He should have lifted up her hand and looked at it, held it admiringly against the light. That no such thing happened was a galling disappointment that Roswitha at once suppressed. I have no bathtub, not even warm running water, she confessed. That didn't deter him, he could install one himself, he said. Then Roswitha suddenly felt what it meant to have a man in the house. And she sent him away so that he could bring his things to her from the shack. As she wiped clean the linoleum in the hall and hurried back to the bedroom, it occurred to her that his eyes were watery blue and his eyelids inflamed.

Max is back again. He is standing outside the door with a cardboard suitcase, a thing covered with scratches, and again Roswitha feels apprehensive for a moment. Soon, though, she is moved with joy: a man is bringing his suitcase to her. That means someone is arriving at her place, someone has been on his way to her, has packed his suitcase on her account, has come the distance to her with this piece of baggage, has lugged it into the house and up the stairs. Now he is putting it down in front of her. Never, it occurs to her now, never before has anyone ever come to me with a suitcase. She is immediately curious: What might it contain? People don't go on trips with anything like that any more, and they also don't move in anywhere with it. But the thing, actually little better than a cardboard box, is now in front of her. Where should it go? There is nothing but dirty laundry in it, says Max. He lugs the container into the kitchen and opens it, revealing a terrible mess. Roswitha bends down to put the items of laundry in order. Max stays standing behind her and looks down at the stooping woman. Finally she stuffs the laundry with the strong smell into the laundry basket, filling it completely. That means that she had best turn on the water-heater in the laundry room tomorrow, heat lye in the laundry tub, boil his laundry, brush it, wring it, spin it ... it would take her half a day. She swallows her displeasure and shows him a place in the corridor for the empty suitcase and also shows him the toilet that doesn't flush, but instead has a heavy wooden lid. The house is old.

He seems to like the bedroom with its light-colored furniture and the beds with their polished brass bars; he looks at the picture over the head end of the double beds, it is the heart of Mary pierced with seven flaming swords, and he smiles and says his knife collection will go really well with that. Max is still carrying a rucksack on his back, he takes it now from his shoulders, throws it on the bed, opens it and pulls out a wooden box that he puts on the little bedside table with the dainty brass legs and the glass plate, opens two small doors, and Roswitha sees knives in it hanging close together in leather loops, knives in various sizes, with different handles and shapes. But all gleaming, neat and tidy, polished. Roswitha doesn't know what to think of them, Max asks her to guess how many there are, she shrugs her shoulders and makes an effort and finally mentions a number: Fifty, she says. Ninety-eight, he crows. What are they for? Roswitha wonders. He plays with them to pass the time, throwing the small knives so that they outline figures when they are stuck in the target. Sometimes he also hurls them at targets in competition. He has developed a certain skill at it. His sure aim is hard to beat. Roswitha doesn't know what to think of her future husband's hobby, but thinks with quiet satisfaction that Max is no ordinary mason; he distinguishes himself from others through his talent. All the same, she doesn't want to learn anything more about it now; later, she thinks and leads him back into the kitchen. There he finishes unpacking his rucksack, bringing to light two pairs of long pants, a clean shirt and underwear.

In Roswitha's kitchen there is only cold running water and that only in the last four years. The installation cost her a tidy sum at the time. Before that she had to fetch every drop of water from the well of the neighboring house fifty meters away. The running water had seemed like a luxury to her for a while, now she was long since used to it and had already begun to think about the cost of a bathtub. She shows Max which pan is used for warming water for washing, which element of the hotplate is used for that, puts out a clean towel and soap for him, pulls out the washbasin from under the counter and puts it on the washstand. Max wants to get washed. Roswitha withdraws to her workshop. His being here has made the kitchen even smaller. When he was familiar with the customs of her household they would no longer be in each other's way. This thought consoles her as she puts a bright cloth and two wine glasses on the sewing table. To go with the wine she puts out a basket of pretzels. Together they drink the whole bottle of Dürnsteiner Katzensprung. That goes quickly, although Max says he is actually a beer drinker. He is also a smoker. That does bother her, but nothing can be done about it. It's still summer and the window can stay open. Max tells about his life. Roswitha listens attentively; she finds everything so confusing, though, that she seems to know less about him afterwards than before. In any case, he gets up at 6 o'clock, because his work begins at 6:30. Roswitha wants to make him breakfast, coffee, or whatever he wants, with rolls or croissants or pretzels. She promises him everything. The wine has its effect. Max has once "come in conflict" with the law, as he expresses it. After that he lost his position as linesman with the railway. And there was a woman, a "slut," involved in it. That remains vaguely in Roswitha's memory, together with an indistinct feeling of sympathy that brings him closer to her.

As soon as she knows Max is in the bedroom, she also makes her way to bed. The smell of nicotine is still hanging in the room and keeps her from getting to sleep for a while. Still, she is convinced that it is better not to be alone in the apartment. Admittedly, the bedroom seems for the time being entirely separated from the rest of the apartment and off limits, a forbidden room, as it were. And she an unauthorized person.

As she lies in bed and can't stop imagining her bedroom, where the sounds of a sleeping person must be audible, she feels a tingling sensation on her skin, just knowing that she is no longer alone. The room that was unoccupied for decades now contains life, in a manner that bewilders her. This room, filled with the sounds of breathing, makes her sleepless, as if the droning of the man's breath and other unimaginable sounds could come over her at night, as soon as she had fallen asleep, and shake her awake; or smells would come; smells, my God, pleasant smells would emanate from his bed and pour themselves on and over her closed eyes, she would be inundated with strange and extraordinary things. She would probably only be able to live with the sound of his breathing and become accustomed to it when she was lying next to him. Then her fear too would disappear.

Roswitha awakes. She thinks she feels someone shaking her shoulder. She jumps up and finds herself alone. Dawn is breaking. Then she hears something clatter. A door has shut or been shut. Then footsteps in the hall and the squeak of the lavatory door. So he is up already. She can't let him see her like this, in her nightgown, with her wild hair. She looks for a dress. Her dressing-gown is too shabby. She tears at her hair with the comb. Now she hears a noise from the kitchen. She gets tangled up in the sleeves of her smock. Again some strands of hair come loose; quickly she pushes a comb into the bun at her neck.

A half glass-paneled door with a flowered curtain over its panes leads from the kitchen into the bedroom. Max isn't in the kitchen yet. First she wants to prepare breakfast, then changes her mind and arranges things so he can get washed. Suddenly Max is standing in front of her, and she is startled. He is already wearing his work pants, but the upper part of his body is naked. Roswitha quickly pushes the pot of water onto the hotplate and wants to run away from the wooly blond frizz on the man's chest. But she stays and puts the washstand in the right place for him. Behind her she hears a bristly rustling that tells her he is scraping over the stubble of his beard. She turns around and presses past him toward the counter, he steps back and now stands squeezed in between the bedroom door and the table. She rummages about in the cupboard for coffee cups and cutlery. She looks past him and asks him to sit down. The water for washing will be ready right away.

When he sits down, thinks Roswitha, I will quickly regain my composure. She shows Max again where to find the towels and soap dish, the washstand and the wash basin. While she is showing him, she gets everything ready. Now and then she casts a glance in his direction. He sits silently, just rubbing his beard and his eyes again and again and running his fingers through his tousled hair. He looks different than he did yesterday, Roswitha finds. He is losing his strangeness. Although his face seems changed to her, she thinks she can find something familiar in it. Overnight the strangeness has changed into a cautious familiarity. He stands up, stretches and shows her his powerful neck and his broad back covered with freckles. She has everything arranged for his morning toilet and regrets again that getting washed in her apartment is so awkward and involved. Max repeats what he had already announced yesterday, he will install a bath. It occurs to Roswitha that her apartment was once a priest's apartment. She wants to entertain him with this story, mainly though to distract herself from his naked upper body and the curly hairs on it. But as he bends over the wash-basin and scoops the water into his face with cupped hands, she draws back.

In her workshop she sits at her sewing machine peculiarly idle and thinks of his sleepy eyes, his body still warm from bed, the hairs on it and the honey colored landscape of freckles on his back. Later she stands up, airs the covers and shakes the sheet out the window over the abandoned scaffolding. It promises to be another sunny late summer day; the lawns are still wet with dew. When was the last time she looked out the window so early? She looks at the lawn of the parish garden enclosed by a wooden fence, and its currant bushes and rose beds. The construction work has beaten a track across the lawn, and three prison guards in moss green uniforms are making use of it. Seen from above, their caps with shields look like the lids of hatboxes that someone clapped on the men's heads in a carnival mood. Roswitha, of course, knows that the guards, who are walking purposefully to work, must wear their regulation uniforms. When one meets them on level ground, the caps do emphasize their authority and make office bearers of the men.

In a more distant part of the garden, between the rosebushes, the priest in his black cassock is praying from the breviary. Roswitha spreads the sheet over the mattress. There is a knock at the door. Leimer shows himself washed. He has even thrown away the dirty water and put away the basin and washstand. Only the puddles still slide around on the linoleum. Roswitha takes the rag out of the side drawer and wipes the floor dry. Then they sit across from each other for the first time over breakfast. She pours the coffee. Max does not take jam. She sits at the narrow side, he at the long side of the table.

He still has not noticed her beautiful hands. Or the delicate way she raises the porcelain cup to her mouth. When she pours more coffee, his eyes are directed at the stream of coffee and not at her hands, although she taps on the belly of the pot with the stretched out index finger of her right hand. Is it possible he can overlook how agilely her fingers coil themselves around the porcelain of the pot and how their white stands out against the dark blue glaze? No, he has no eyes for that. So it doesn't come as a surprise to her that he slurps his coffee and munches down the bread and butter loudly and absent-mindedly. While he is eating he holds his head bowed low, so that she has the part in his hair before her eyes. White flaky skin shows through the hair that probably used to be reddish blond but has gone gray. Roswitha gets a heavy heart. Later they discuss household expenses, in this matter they quickly come to an agreement. That lets Roswitha hope again. And Max goes right into the bedroom and comes back with his purse, from which he forks over the money. He freely opens the billfold in front of her. In it she sees that he also has several larger bills. He snaps the wallet shut and deposits it again in the bedroom.

With that, it is time for Max to go to work.

Roswitha ponders her situation. Someone has left her apartment and gone to his place of work. He has also left his cash behind with her. He will come back. He will be with her again at noon. And every day from today on. From now on I have to cook for a man, she says to herself and is almost frightened; he needs something substantial that gives him strength and endurance, and it must be well seasoned. Roswitha is not prepared for that. She leaves her other work undone and leafs through the cookbook. For a while she forgets everything else, including that she wants to tell her sister something of her marriage plans.

In the bedroom the window is still open. She must ask Max

whether the rushing sound of the river disturbed him and whether he heard the chiming of the clock in the church steeple. Roswitha wants to make the bed for Max. That is the proper thing, she finds. But the place where he slept is already in order. He has smoothed down the pillow and the quilt. That makes her think. What does it mean that he has made his own bed? Is it because he as a polite person wants to relieve her of work, to burden her as little as possible? Or is he giving her to understand that his bed is no concern of hers? Is he sending the unspoken message: keep away from me?

She could use some advice right away. Lotte, who knows men, would know what to say. Roswitha opens the doors of the wardrobe. Max has put some underwear and two plaid shirts on the shelves. A loden green coat is hanging on a hanger and a pair of brown pants with frayed tail braid and torn pockets. That would be something for her. She would like to have taken the pants out of the wardrobe right away and seated herself at the sewing machine with them. She doesn't dare to do so though before she asks him. After all he did make his own bed. She closes the wardrobe door again and looks out the window. The river, the hills, the meadow landscape lie before her, and below her the narrow path along the river lined with willow trees. Perhaps it wasn't wise to do without this room. She could like it here: the view, the light. The bedroom has sun from morning to noon. Did the priest use it as his study when he lived here? It surprises her more and more that she neglected the room all these years. And now she has relinquished it.

Roswitha remembers her sister. She drops everything and gets on her way. A talk with Martha seems to her to be the most important thing right now. Her sister lives on a hill a little way from the village, in a single family house she and her husband toiled and saved for. In the small front garden all kinds of flowers are blooming, and ornamental bushes grow along the narrow walkway to the house. She has everything she can wish for, thinks Roswitha. Her own house with garden, a husband with a secure civil service job at the post office, and a son who works for a transport company in the capital city and has a good chance of being promoted to management. That is the framework in which happiness likes to show itself. Martha opens the door for her sister and is surprised. So early in the morning, at such an unusual time. That has to startle her. You should have phoned, says Martha, I'm not at all prepared for company. Martha always acts as if she didn't know that Roswitha doesn't have a phone. It's incomprehensible to her how a businesswoman, and you are a businesswoman, strictly speaking, can get along without a phone.

All in due time, says Roswitha and smiles. What's up, asks Martha, you are grinning and rubbing your hands. Are you planning something? Martha stays standing in the narrow corridor and eyes her sister. Roswitha would have liked to sit down comfortably with her in the living room, perhaps drink a cup of coffee, a ceremony that would have made it easier for her to tell her sister everything. Yes, Roswitha answers, I am planning something. Martha sighs and says, then we'll just go into the kitchen, we can't stay standing here, and then you can tell me what's on your mind. The kitchen has not been cleared up; there are dirty dishes on the counter. On the only chair there is a pile of laundry. Martha takes the pile and puts it on the window ledge. Sit down. Roswitha, who actually doesn't want to sit down, sits down. She has to concentrate entirely on the words with which she now wants to tell Martha the news. Martha stays standing at the window and looks at her sister. Martha was always strict with her, probably because of the age difference of twelve years. She also already has some gray hair that Roswitha notices today for the first time. She is an old woman she thinks immediately and is ashamed of her thought, as if she had spoken badly of her sister to others. Roswitha feels suddenly young and somehow like a bride. She bursts out: I have a man. That was the wrong sentence and naturally led to misunderstandings with Martha, because Martha laughed, she couldn't stop laughing for a long time. That hurt Roswitha's ears and heart. Martha excused herself and said she had almost peed in her pants, she didn't know why she had had to laugh that way, there was nothing to laugh about if her sister had a man, and Roswitha saw the corners of Martha's mouth twitching again as she was fighting back a new fit of laughter. I mean, says Roswitha, who for her part is struggling to keep back the tears, I am going to marry. At last Martha gets herself under control, and her face looks suddenly tired and sad from all the laughter. Roswitha finally finds a sentence to which she can connect the story she has worked out: that they have been writing letters to each other for quite some time, and that Max arranged to be transferred to her neighborhood and moved in with her yesterday. Then Martha becomes suspicious and asks: So quickly? Without further ado? And you wrote letters?

> -Yes, wrote letters.
> -And already moved in with you?
> -Into the bedroom, just into the bedroom.
> -Into the bedroom?
> -Yes.
> -A stranger has moved into our parents' bedroom?
> -I am going to marry him.
> -Marry?
> -Yes.
> -When?
> -Soon.
> -How soon?
> -Just soon.

Martha still hasn't moved away from the window. She shakes her head. Then she shrugs her shoulders and sighs.

> -I don't understand you, says Roswitha sheepishly and feels that she is about to cry.
> -It's alright, says Martha, you are old enough. Have to know yourself what you are doing.

No one can advise you or help you.

Roswitha gets up. Martha goes to the kitchen cupboard, takes out a bottle of cognac and two glasses. We have to drink to this, she says and fills both glasses to the brim.

> -I'm not drinking any cognac, and certainly not in broad daylight, Roswitha refuses. Her sister has already tipped

down the first glass, she holds the second out to Roswitha. Roswitha doesn't say another word, turns around and leaves the kitchen, goes through the corridor and out of the house. I have nothing more to say to her, she thinks, as she closes the garden gate behind her. Then she feels better. It's not good to pay visits so early in the morning, she says as she walks along. In the afternoon everything might have taken a different course.

On the way home she does her shopping in the grocery store. She has a long shopping list today. Leokadia Braml, the grocer woman, is noticeably surprised by the unusual quantity of cold cuts, bread and cheese that Roswitha orders. Company? she asks.

Roswitha feels herself flush and she knows her face is now full of red blotches. Yes, she nods and has to clear her throat, a visitor. Really unexpected, from far away? Braml pries. Under her dark eyebrows her eyes lust for news.

Not this way, thinks Roswitha, and not now. Her face cools down again. She wasn't about to give up her own secret; people would have to find out for themselves. Besides, you don't talk about your bridegroom between pickled gherkins, roasted meats, loaves of bread and the cheese dome. Then, in the grip of high spirits, she proceeds to order a cut of roast flank and also takes some curd cheese spread. But then the total amount of the bill does give her a shock.

The grocer woman opens the door for Roswitha. She has heavy parcels to carry. The shopkeeper is prepared to send a female apprentice to help her. But Roswitha declines with thanks.

Despite the heavy load she is struggling with, she allows herself a little detour past Gustav Wondrak's beauty salon. Through the window she can see glossy photos of beautiful women with stylish hairdos. Behind them a large-meshed curtain shields the customers from the gaze of passers-by. Roswitha doesn't dare to stand long in front of the salon window. She is afraid of being observed from inside through the mesh of the curtain.

She acts as if she came past purely by chance, and furtively studies the photos of the hairdos. A dark-haired model has ringlets all over. A reddish-blond model has a page-boy cut that looks as if it was drawn with a ruler. The bangs come right down to her eyebrows and the hair at the sides stops above her earlobes. The hair of a blond model looks as if she had been out in a storm. Roswitha is baffled. None of the hairdos seems to have anything even remotely to do with her. But then again, she thinks as she continues on, she has never encountered anyone with one of the hairdos pictured here. Roswitha decides that the creations in the photos were probably done for individual models and not intended for the ordinary person. Perhaps the curly hairstyle, with a more moderate cut and fullness, would be something for her.

When Roswitha gets back to her house, the word "devastation" comes to mind. She whispers it to herself in horror.

While she was gone, the front part of the building has been completely surrounded by scaffolding and the plaster knocked off, leaving the wall looking scabby. There are piles of sand, cement and gravel in front; mixing machines, wire netting, tools; just then a truck makes a shrill sound dumping another load of sand. It seems that everything has been unleashed today. Everything seems bent on destruction. There is even a Caterpillar tractor digging its way through the opened wrought-iron gates of the parish garden. Several work jackets and beer bottles are lying on the ground under the walnut tree. The men are all in motion. In her haste to get to the house she cannot discover Max in all the confusion.

It's very noisy in the apartment too. She hears the mixing machines grinding, trucks driving back and forth, gravel rumbling; she feels the floor and walls vibrating from the noise. She thinks of Max doing his duty out there in this infernal commotion, working with all his might on the improvement of her house. So for him she has to make a hearty, tasty meal that should not only fill his stomach but also please him. Therefore, she cooks smoked meat, dumplings and sauerkraut. The extensive menu makes her perspire. Again and again, she has to interrupt kneading the dumplings and seasoning the food to look something up in the cookbook. It's been a long time since she made semolina dumplings, who knows if they'll be a success. They have to be light and creamy and able to be cut with a fork.

On the stroke of twelve, the noise outside dies down. There is ringing and knocking at the door. That's Max. Roswitha has the door to the apartment locked. Perhaps she should give him a key, so that he feels at home at her place more quickly.

Max is dusty and sweaty and is standing in front of her with his upper body naked asking for a wash-basin. The request is understandable. But on the stove the dumplings, the soup, and the smoked meat with the sauerkraut are steaming in the pots. Also, the table is already set. Where, in this confined space, is there room for the washstand and washbasin! In the end, Roswitha carries the wash table with the basin into the hall, brings him a jug of cold water – he did specifically request cold water --, and also provides him with a towel and soap. She retreats behind the glass wall into the kitchen. For her there is nothing more to do but wait. She casts fleeting glances over Max's back as he leans forward. With his hands, he is shoveling the water into his face and over his chest with it splashing everywhere. She thinks of the puddles she will have to wipe up from the linoleum.

Through the pane of glass she indicates to the man that he can just leave everything where it is. So he comes smiling to the table and nods. His hair is moist at his temples and at the nape of his neck. The blond hair on his chest, which looks like dense wooly smoke after being rubbed with the towel, rattles Roswitha. It isn't proper, she thinks. In the confined space between the pots, the smoked meat, the soup, and the dumplings that turned out well, there is no article of clothing that she could have put on him. Her father never sat at the table stripped to the skin like that. He at least wore a cotton undershirt. And now this stranger is already sitting across from her at their first mealtime with his curly chest hairs. Leimer obviously feels comfortable in his nakedness. Here in the dark arched kitchen he can cool his hot body. Roswitha has understanding for that.

The meal tastes good to him. He takes large helpings. During the meal, he doesn't look up from his plate. Roswitha finds herself and her place setting pushed into the background, because Leimer's elbows take up a lot of room when he is cutting the meat, dividing the dumplings and having a second helping. She tries to get him to look up by starting a conversation. Wasn't it very hot at work today, she wants to know. She has to repeat her question, because he doesn't respond. He raises his head and makes a vague, far-reaching movement with his arm that is perhaps supposed to imply that it could be worse, or that it's bearable, or that it just has to be accepted.

After finishing his meal he puts his knife and fork on the plate, pushes it away from himself and lights a cigarette, after first uttering more as a statement than a question: you don't mind if I smoke, do you. Now he also stretches out his legs under the table. He looks Roswitha in the face a few times, grins and blows the smoke out his nose. Roswitha remains seated. If she got up now and cleared away the plates as she usually does, the opportunity would be lost. She would scare him away if she leapt up after the meal and scraped and splashed at the pots. She has caught his smile, that's what she was waiting for. She observed him, stared in his face while he was lighting his cigarette. Over the flickering of the match his face reddened, and through the flame she looked under his bony blond eyebrows into his eyes, looked through his uneven eyelashes, like through a fence, into his blue-gray pupils. He looks up again. She yearns for a second smile. He would have to say something; whatever it was, she would take it up and develop it into a thread of conversation; she was determined not to let him fall silent any more. She runs her hands apparently unintentionally over her temples. Over her forehead she spreads out her fingers with the rising moons under the nails. He is long since somewhere else with his eyes, perhaps on the ceiling; he has tipped his head back and is blowing smoke at the whitewashed dome. Roswitha decides to say something, no matter what happens. But then he stands up, lifts his hand in a brief greeting and goes back to work. He leaves behind his wash water for her, the puddles on the floor, and the dirty dishes. As Roswitha is carrying the washbasin into the kitchen, she suddenly remembers her sister again, and in sudden anger she pours the water so violently into the drain that it sloshes back over her legs.

Roswitha is dead tired, but she can't fall asleep. During the day she sometimes thought longingly of her bed and looked forward to a night's sleep. The day was very stressful for her. She didn't even have her usual time off at lunch, because there was sewing that urgently needed her attention, and later it was already time for her to prepare the evening meal. Besides, the waiting for Max had exhausted her. Because he didn't come. The sight of the deserted construction sight confused her. The disappearance of her tenant dismayed her. After all, he had come up the narrow stairs and come to her place the day before yesterday, or had it just been yesterday, with dirty hands and his clothing stiff with dust. So she expected it would be like that today, too, and thought she could expect that every day. But Max didn't come. The piles of cement and gravel lie abandoned. The caterpillar tractor is immobilized with its shovel drawn in. Max and the others have gone, without Roswitha noticing. If only she had looked out the window as she had felt the urge to do when the mixing machines, motors, shoveling and hammering noises stopped! She would have seen the workers leaving in different directions, she could have traced Leimer's steps which had led him away from her house instead of to it; she could have called out to him to ask where he was going. She could also have hurried down the steps, run after him and breathed her fear down his neck, or she could have remained calm and stared after his steps from behind the windowpane. But perhaps, if she had been standing at the window at the right moment, Max would have looked up to her and called to her. Coming right away! Or something like that. Instead, Roswitha set the table. And then she sat at the hall window, where she had an overview of the road, and waited. Gradually the conviction took hold in her that he would never come back again. He had come from the dust, and now he was gone, the dust was settling behind him, she thought, and could have laughed at the play on words. But she didn't feel at all like laughing. On the contrary. She thought of the missing bathroom and the toilet that was just a hole in boards: all good reasons to leave. Or she herself, the crippled woman, why should he stay with her? He had found another place to stay. After all, she even seemed to herself like a cage, filled up to the bars with loneliness.

Then she saw him at the elderberry bush, and saw that he was coming home. He had been at the pub. Previously he had gone to the pub first thing after work every day. The evening only began for him with the pub. He wasn't defending himself, he just let her know it. And immediately after that her feeling of shame: How ridiculously she had behaved to herself! Thank God no one had seen her fear. What wouldn't she have been prepared to give for him in those two hours of waiting, to have him come back again! And now that he was here, all dirty and stinking of cigarette smoke, she no longer wanted to remember her feelings of black despair.

He was getting washed. How could she have forgotten that he was used to getting washed before the meal. Roswitha had already quickly put the food out again. Again she got out the necessary things for him to wash in the corridor. Tomorrow I will know better, tomorrow I won't bring the food to the table until he has washed, every day will be a little less awkward. So she thinks, as she lies awake. They ate, it tasted good to him, and he hardly spoke and didn't ask her anything. He also didn't notice the beauty of her hands. She examines her hands against the moonlight. Even the most resentful people can have no doubts about the beauty of her hands. She herself has never seen such well-formed hands; sometimes, in pictures of female saints, she has found similarly formed hands. Her own were every bit as beautiful as those in the pictures. Even Leimer would some day have to notice her hands. Whether he would hold them in his own without saying a word, there probably weren't many words to be expected from his mouth, or whether he would stroke them, perhaps even massage them or kiss them! Of course he is still sleeping like a log while she, who is overtired, can't get to sleep.

She slips out of bed and stands at the window. This silence, she thinks, and the church across the way, the two onion towers show me their rear side, and the nave lies before my eyes in its entire length. There is no house that is closer to the church, to this baroque jewel, as it is called in all the schoolbooks, and no house closer to the penitentiary. The prison wing, an old monastery building, is an annex to the nave. Roswitha waits for the clock in the tower to strike twelve. That gives her a pleasant shudder, as does the thought that the tolling of the bell would also be heard by the prisoners, at least by those who like her can't sleep, behind their cell windows with the dark yellow light shining on them. At night two guards are on patrol behind the barbed-wire fence, walking casually like civilians. There are also floodlights on the towers. The verdigris patina of their copper roofs stands out against the bright ray of light and the night sky. After the sound of the clock striking midnight has died away, their illumination is extinguished. The floodlights remain on the penitentiary all night. Roswitha hears the rushing sound of the river as she leans out the window. Max is obviously not bothered by it in his sleep. How would the river sound in his room, mixed with the sleeper's breathing? She would like to know that. What is keeping her from surreptitiously finding out? After all, it is her apartment where all that is happening. And if he were to catch her at it? An excuse would probably quickly be found. But he wouldn't wake up. He already slept deeply the first night he was there, as he proudly asserted, he would do the same tonight. But she wants to see him sleeping. Wants to know how he looks when he is asleep and how he sounds and how, indeed, if he moves in her parents' marriage-bed.

She wants to sneak into the bedroom through the corridor, not through the kitchen that would take her right to the head end of his bed. That would be too dangerous. She wants to approach him from the foot end. In the dark she gropes her way along the corridor, feels her way along the wall – the endless, disgustingly dusty wall – to the door. At last she feels the smooth wood, the door, her hands run over it looking for the handle. Much too loudly. I had better flit back, she thinks. But she stays standing in the darkness, breathing quickly and listening. Nothing moves. The door can be opened without a sound. With the moonlight shining into the room, everything is recognizable: the wardrobe and the dressing table with the three-part mirror, the heater in the corner with the long black stovepipe, the night tables and the wide bed with the man in it. And the small box with his knives. Roswitha leaves the door open and ventures a step into the room. The floor boards creak. The river is rushing more loudly than she remembers it, as if it were high water; or is the rushing sound in her ears? Max Leimer is lying on the bed like a fat caterpillar, wrapped in the quilt. Over the swirling of the water she hears an unfamiliar sound, his breathing out and breathing in, it splutters, falls silent and bubbles again. She ventures yet another step toward the bed. His head is lying on the hard feather pillow that he has rolled up. At first she sees only the back of his head and his tousled hair. She wants to see his face though. The sleeper doesn't move. A corner of the quilt shades the front view of him so that she can only make it out very indistinctly no matter how boldly she approaches him, coming so close that his breath is whistling in her face and she can feel it stroking her cheeks. His eye sockets are black under his forehead, the ridge of his nose gleams brightly, and on his half-closed lips, actually on his lower lip there are little drops of saliva. She bends even closer to him. Max snorts. His breath seems to assault her mouth and chin. She staggers back. Then the sleeping man jerks. His arms reach out with a mighty swing, there is movement and thrashing under the quilt, Max is rolling over onto his other side. His feet shove themselves through the brass bars. His head burrows under the pillow as if he suspects that he is being observed. Roswitha stumbles away, his breath still moist on her lips. As she hurries past, she catches sight of her shadowy figure in the mirror and escapes into the corridor. Shivering, she crawls into bed and now she really can't sleep. Perhaps she would go there again tomorrow. Perhaps she would dare to stroke his cheek with her fingertips or touch his eyelids with tips of her fingers. Perhaps she would hold the palms of her hands in his breath. Perhaps he would have beautiful dreams if she stroked his forehead, and he would put his arms around her in his dream. I'm crazy, thinks Roswitha, I am really silly. And yet she makes plans: Tomorrow I'll go to the hairdresser and get a new hairdo.

It is only the third morning that they are eating breakfast together, entering from different doors and going toward each other, sitting at the table, and already there are signs of something like habit. Roswitha is afraid of it; their relationship is already threatening to petrify before it has come alive. He is acting as if he had already reached his goal. He has moved into his quarters; he hardly notices the quarter mistress, the woman who is giving him quarters. He finds nothing lacking. So she herself has to go to work. She has to remain lively, get his attention, tickle him, wake him up. She tries again today to make conversation. He doesn't raise his head from his coffee cup until she asks a second time, calling him by name: Max, did you sleep well?

I always sleep well.

Doesn't the moon bother you? The moon would shine through those thin curtains. Roswitha tries to make a joke: I hope you don't start sleepwalking, or are you already a sleepwalker and don't know it and have already stood on the windowsill and even gone for a walk on the ledge?

Nonsense, answers Max, I fall into bed and am asleep, moon or no moon. I have to be sick not to be able to sleep at night.

His tone leaves no doubt that his sound sleep is a virtue on which he prides himself. Roswitha seems ridiculous to herself and remains silent. Still, Leimer said something, he told about himself, about a particular characteristic, used it to praise himself to her: a man, thinks Roswitha, who sleeps like the dead, if that isn't something!

Yes, yes, says Roswitha, one sleeps best with a clear conscience.

Indeed, answers Max.

As the hairdresser tilts Roswitha's head carefully back, Roswitha is pleased that she has acted on her decision.

Is it right like this? asks the girl as she lathers Roswitha's hair and massages her scalp.

Yes, yes, Roswitha assures her.

We need a permanent wave. Our hair is too fine, says the hairdresser.

Roswitha nods: I know.

It also gets oily quickly, says the assistant, and rubs Roswitha's hair between her fingertips.

Yes, unfortunately, sighs Roswitha.

So we have to make it shorter. We need a haircut, layered, but not too short, so that we still have some fullness, especially at the back of the head, explains the expert.

I will rely entirely on you, declares Roswitha.

Maybe also some bangs on your forehead, sloping like this, from left to right, a stylish wave?

Whatever you think.

Well then, we'll try it, smiles the assistant with the little name plate Petra on her yellow smock.

Now Miss Petra's fingertips are massaging Roswitha's scalp, they circle around over her temples and down the back of her head to her neck. That feels good. She will grant herself this pleasure more often now. She keeps her eyes shut; the hairdresser's hands are stroking the lather again and again from her forehead and temples. This morning, Roswitha remembers now, Lotte was standing unexpectedly at her door. Unexpected and unwelcome. Roswitha remembers that to her frustration she blushed. I felt caught, she thinks. It was embarrassing for me that Lotte might discover that I have a man living with me. Fortunately, Lotte didn't notice anything. She was thinking only about her play and wanted to talk about it. She had embraced her friend and hugged her and blathered on about a fateful discussion. Well, she too, thought Roswitha to herself, fateful times must be hanging in the air. A fine and educated person he was, the school inspector, an artist! Roswitha nodded. He has written a play, something dramatic, you know. Roswitha nodded again and waited. He has offered me the lead role in his play, me! cried Lotte enthusiastically. Roswitha asked what and whom she was supposed to play and what type of play it was, what it was about. Something comical? That, Lotte waves the question impatiently aside, she doesn't exactly know yet. Something historical on any account. For her, the only thing of importance was: the lead role. Even as a child she had always liked to act, even in school, which is what the inspector remembered. He had been the senior primary school teacher at that time. The inspector had spoken of her talent for acting that he had noticed back then. You should be my heroine, he had exclaimed. Heroine in his play, he meant. Then Lotte presented Roswitha with a list of signatures, or rather a call for donations. Financial support of the theatrical project "1000 Years G."

Roswitha, still under the hairdresser's comfortable hands, remembers that she put her name and her signature on the list and gave a financial contribution. She is now leading the list with her name and the sum of money. Lotte left soon afterwards. She said, as she draped the red silk shawl around her neck, that she still had to be grateful to her for her signature and donation, but soon, she was convinced of this, her friend would thank her, because the culture would ennoble her existence. With this vague promise, Lotte ran down the stairs. The shawl fluttered over her shoulder. Roswitha laughed out loud. Her friend had been funny. How she suddenly expressed herself! That was probably a result of her dealings with the school inspector. That's off to a good start, Roswitha had thought.

Even now, at the thought of it, she smiles, while Miss Petra has begun the procedure with the pungent-smelling lotions. It continues with curlers, waiting, rinsing, curlers, waiting, drying, waiting.

The girl supplies her customer with magazines. Roswitha leafs through them absent-mindedly. She is surrounded by mirrors. She is mirrored from behind, from in front and from the sides. As the rollers are taken out of her hair, she doesn't take her eyes off herself. She observes Petra, whose face is mirrored over hers, working seriously, as it seems to Roswitha and that flatters her, giving shape to her hair. The plucking, backcombing, brushing and arranging of individual strands of hair over her forehead, behind her ears and at her neck tickles Roswitha so gently that she wishes the hairdresser would not be finished for a long time. But much too quickly and abruptly the girl's hands remove themselves at last from her hair. As if by magic, Petra produces a hand mirror behind her back and uses it to project the back view of the hairdo onto the big mirror in front of Roswitha. Does it suit you like that? asks the assistant after a little while. Roswitha nods in lively agreement. She pays the bill, which seems a lot to her. That includes several things, she thinks, and goes out of the store feeling as if a light gust of wind could make her head float away like a balloon. On her way home she can't resist looking at her reflection in the store windows. She likes what she sees, even if she does have the impression somewhat that people could take her hair for a wig. The hairdo is still foreign to her face, even if it does form a friendly frame around it. Nevertheless, she determines with satisfaction that her nose seems more delicate and her mouth softer and fuller.

She has succeeded in attracting his attention. He comes home late, like yesterday. She already has everything ready for him. Even at the door he hesitates. He looks at her uncertainly, but says nothing, turns away, looks at her again. I hardly recognized you, he says at last. Roswitha makes a hasty little gesture toward the fullness at the back of her head: I've been at the hairdresser's.

Aha, he says relieved, a new hairdo! He laughs heartily, but nothing else occurs to him.

Then everything goes its already accustomed way.

They eat together, he stays sitting at the table a little and smokes. Then he starts to talk: The work is hard. I used to have a nice job. And an important one at that. He had been a linesman. The walking in the fresh air, the freedom that he once felt is lacking now, he misses moving forwards.

Roswitha takes up that point: How would it be then if they went for a walk on the weekend, if he liked to walk so much, she thought, perhaps they could go together. At first he doesn't answer, and Roswitha fears he has fallen completely silent again. But then he raises his head and looks at her thoughtfully: What, you would want to go along?

Of course, she says inadvertently, why not?

He gets matter-of-fact: How long do you think you will be able to keep up with me? How many kilometers, I mean.

My God, Roswitha is surprised, I don't know that. On the hill at the edge of town it is very pretty. People can rest on the benches between the crab apple trees, or stop at the farmer's for a glass of fruit wine.

That's not what Max had in mind. He says so right away. He wants to walk on the ties of the railway tracks, like he used to. Between the rails of the narrow-gauge railway. He could show her how to walk on the ties. She would be astonished how quickly a person moves forward on them. He would feel the trains – the few that still travel on this track – in good time. He has a sixth sense for their approach. Roswitha looks down at herself. She looks at her crippled foot. So she with her infirmity, has he really not noticed her infirmity, is supposed to go to all this effort? But is it wise to refuse his offer? Perhaps when she is holding on to his arm it will be possible to get closer to him. If she doesn't keep up with him, she'll just have to turn back. And besides, no one would see them, or hardly anyone. Granted, some single family dwellings stand quite close to the tracks. And if someone from the town were to recognize her, to see her arm in arm with Leimer, a strange man, on or between the rails ... who knows what the people would think. Wouldn't they think she was crazy, or at least weary of life, and try to take her away by force? She tells Max her fear. He, however, obsessed with the idea of carrying out his former job at least as a hobby, is not to be dissuaded. We'll seek out the quiet places and go back and forth. He knew the area. There were long stretches of forest near by, they could do some practicing there, as he called it; after such a long time he would have to regain his former agility and technique. Then Roswitha has no more objections. Gradually, she even begins to take a lively interest in his suggestion. Going back and forth in a small forest! Arm in arm! She is already looking forward to the outing. At least something has got under way – in the truest sense of the word. She can be satisfied.

Then they wish each other a good night and go to bed. Today too, as every evening since he has been there, Roswitha is unable to fall asleep. She hears the clock in the tower strike. So she has already been lying awake in bed an hour. Max has probably long since been asleep.

As she creeps out of bed in order to sneak to his bed again, she already feels she has a right to do that. The dark corridor is more quickly traversed, the door handle surely found. She kneels at his bed and freely observes his shaded face, which consists of dark valleys and the bright ridge of the bridge of his nose, faintly modeled by the moonlight. And the sounds of his breathing, the blowing from his nose, the breath from his mouth! She kneels huddled together and dimly senses rather than sees the gentle widening of his nostrils, and when the sound of his breath changes to a slightly rattling, higher pitch, his lower lip trembles.

She stays until her legs start to hurt. Now she has difficulty getting up without making a noise, because she has become quite stiff from the unaccustomed position and her feet are numb. She feels her way around the bed. She is tempted to see how it feels to lie next to him, how she likes the marital bed. What if she tried to slip herself onto the mattress at his side? But what if this movement startled him and woke him up? How would she explain her being there to him? Carefully she presses on the mattress to see if it would make a sound, and slips onto the bed that now does creak a little. She turns onto her back and looks at the ceiling, where the cross-bars of the window appear in silhouette, hears the river and feels Leimer's presence. She doesn't dare turn her head to his side.

One day I will fall asleep beside him, she thinks fervently, and every day after that. Now she does turn her head slowly in his direction on the firm mattress. It surprises her that he crawls under the stuffed quilt on these mild late summer nights, so that hardly his shock of hair or even a foot protrudes. Does he sleep naked, or is he wearing pajamas? It is unimaginable that anyone with clothes on could stand it under the quilt, bathed in sweat one has to wake up at some point. But Max is sleeping, as long as she lies beside him on the mattress, almost without moving. Tomorrow she will look for pajamas in his bed. If he doesn't have any, that explains his crawling under the quilt so that it covers even the hair on his head. Roswitha never sleeps naked. The idea would never have occurred to her. She even wears underwear under her nightgown. Sometimes it helps her fall asleep if she puts her hands between her thighs, but she has always felt the smooth jersey material instead of the wool of her pubic hair. The thought that Max is lying naked beside her under the quilt excites her. It tickles her pleasantly and she asks herself in bewilderment whether she is allowed to have such a feeling and who knows where that might lead with her. She gets out of there fast, lustfully pursued by a feeling of revulsion.

I won't come back any more, she swears to herself. It isn't proper. And there is still so much to be clarified, and underwear to buy for him, if need be pajamas.

The next morning Roswitha searches for pajamas in his cupboard and then in his bed. He has made it again and smoothed it himself. She slides her hands carefully under the pillow and under the quilt, lifting both a little; in the middle of the bed her hands find a warm hollow. Both her hands feel their way around in this pit, there are no pajamas to be found.

Roswitha has become accustomed to the hot late summer days. Even yesterday evening nothing indicated that the weather would take a turn for the worse. Rain and a sudden drop in temperature have taken her by surprise. She stands in front of the opened wardrobe looking for woolen clothing. For now, she has no further use for the light blouses she has worn in the past weeks. Overnight the landscape has become desolate. Now what will become of the walk they had planned? Roswitha is cold. The colors have dimmed, the world has gone gray. She moans.

Right after Sunday breakfast Max reaffirms his decision, in spite of the sudden fall in temperature, to go for a walk along the railway ties. He had often gone to work in rain and wind; he never let bad weather keep him from his duty. Then there is also no going back for Roswitha. She gets a warm jacket and firm shoes ready. She is additionally equipped with an umbrella, so the outing cannot be a failure.

She cooks the meal. Max waits in the workshop. Her hands flutter excitedly. She hopes that he has become absorbed in the newspaper and won't get impatient. Right after breakfast he made his bed and then stood around watching Roswitha closely as she cleared up. I'm ready, he said time after time. That made Roswitha nervous. So she sent him into her workshop with a bottle of beer and the newspaper. He's still sitting there and perhaps drumming irritably on the tabletop with his knuckles.

Finally the food is on the table. Max likes the Wiener schnitzel. The light is on in the kitchen. Outside gray clouds are bringing wet weather.

After the meal Max can hardly be held back. But Roswitha asserts herself; first, she decides, the dishes have to be done, as she is accustomed to doing. Max stays in the kitchen and doesn't let her out of his sight. He himself, of course, does not offer to help. She doesn't dare to go as far as to ask him to dry dishes. Finally the work is done, and Roswitha feels weak. She longs for a little break, a short rest. But she doesn't dare say that out loud.

The open spaces in front of the house, the road, the lawn are ravaged by the construction machinery and the work being done:

soil softened by clay mud puddles, dripping motors and pieces of equipment hidden under black tarpaulins. Their meadow with the gooseberry bushes, the smooth, firmly trodden little path is churned up and boggy.

Max marches happily ahead. He is used to such surroundings, has probably seen worse. Roswitha's shorter leg pushes into the softened soil up to her instep. The firm shoes will withstand the wetness and the dirt a while yet, she hopes. She sees the back of the man quickly hurrying along ahead of her, because the narrow path does not leave room for them to walk beside each other. He is breaking the path, so to speak, she has to walk in his footsteps, and she is glad to duck behind his back. His back is still the most familiar thing about him; this wide back like a tiled oven would probably give off heat in the winter if she rubbed herself against him.

They have long since left the narrow, sodden path, but Max still hasn't turned around to wait for her. In this manner they come to the village square they have to cross. The rain and the midday hour have swept the square clear of people. With Max still straight ahead of her, Roswitha peeks out from under her umbrella, wishing it were as big as a tent. Faces lurk behind the windows; people would be smiling at their strange procession from above. Roswitha can't catch up to Max. The rapid walking is an effort for her; already her hips and thighs are aching. Finally she calls his name. He doesn't hear her until the second time. He does stand still and let her approach. Now she makes an effort to stay at his side. Beside each other they leave the square.

Max walks as if he were following a scent. He walks along the avenue of chestnut trees without hesitation, turns left into a side street, hurries through it, hikes through the settlement with the single family dwellings. Roswitha is no longer surprised and no longer asks where he is going. She follows him blindly. Suddenly he takes a sharp turn to the right and comes to a track across the fields. Evidently he is now heading for the railway embankment that is covered with undergrowth. Roswitha stays behind him. There is no surface on the street now, and she steps into mushy soil. She sees the soles of his shoes ahead of her, with clay around the edges; with his firm, silent steps he makes a track for her, and she sinks down deep in it in her shoes. Then he starts to climb the railway embankment. But he slips, falls to his knees and slides down a bit on his knees. From a strangely contorted position, clutching the undergrowth, he calls over his shoulder to Roswitha: Watch out! She has hesitantly remained standing at the boundary hedge and is tempted to laugh. Max gets up and wipes the clay off his shoes. He now zigzags his way up the embankment with the necessary caution and doesn't fall again. Roswitha, who has refrained from laughing, wipes her shoes free of clay as well and starts to climb the embankment. It turns out, strangely enough, that her handicap proves advantageous to her on the slope. She places her shorter leg between the uphill bushes and then pushes herself up jerkily with her longer leg. On the slope she isn't lame any more. While before her eyes Max had slipped, kneeled, fallen, and had to catch himself in the bushes, she succeeds in conquering the slope in an upright position.

But now they stand before their actual task, walking on the ties. Max doesn't wait any longer, he marches off, turns around once more, calls to her: Watch out! Then she is and remains behind him again. At first she tries to learn the technique of going forward by watching him, but soon she gives that up because she has to concentrate on the ties, on the different distances between them, in order not to fall or stumble or step into the granite breach between the ties. She tries to find out how to do it on her own. It is not as difficult as she had imagined. She considers every step, weighs every distance; then, when she stands on the weaker foot and tries to reach the next tie with her healthy foot, it is a great effort for her to balance on her weak leg. The rails go up a hill in a wide curve and enter a little stand of trees above the village that is simply called the "height."

It's going better than she had feared. Of course she can't keep up with Max. His back, that did seem friendly to her, but also awkward and rigid, has now gotten something springy about it. His spine and his hips have become flexible. He bounces and wriggles forwards, only his neck remains stiff. His knee joints spring back easily when the ties lie farther apart, when they lie close together his legs swing stiffly forward. A dancing tie traverser, thinks Roswitha, he's exaggerating.

The distance is growing between them. She rests to catch her breath and watches him until he has disappeared in the little stand of trees. If only he had turned around to look at her at least once and had observed or even praised her progress forward that was not so clumsy at all! Now she doesn't see him any more, the little stand of trees has swallowed him up. If she reached the grove of beech trees, she would probably be able to see his figure again in the distance, perhaps he was waiting for her after all. A longer, straight stretch runs through the woods, and he must be visible on it, even if only as a little point. So she makes an effort to go faster. That places her under undue stress, because in her haste she almost falls, comes down with her weak foot in the granite breach, and the stones hurt the soles of her feet. When she pauses, straightens up, recovers from the horror of having almost fallen, she sees that she is all alone. The rails before her and behind her lie silent. It's raining, and there is no one to be seen on the streets, in the gardens. Only in the distance, on the through road, cars are whizzing along. Her hands are moist and blotchy. They have lost their uniform pallor. She is cold. It is senseless to go farther into the woods after him, to follow him, to look for him. It's more sensible to turn around and go home. Maybe he would come to his senses on the meadow, becoming concerned when she didn't show up, and he would wait for her between the trees after all. Then he would run back to look for her, and everything would be fine again.

Now she climbs down the embankment the same way she came up it. Though she now uses the umbrella as a cane. It's raining on her new hairdo. Who knows how the curls will react. She feels her way forward with her healthy leg and supports herself on the umbrella.
She gets down successfully.

Again and again she turns around to see if Leimer has come walking out of the woods. Then she is on the main street and the houses block her view of the tracks.

She goes splashing up the stairs in her building with her dirty shoes, chunks of clay smack on the linoleum in her hall.

She has never entered the apartment with such dirty shoes. As soon as she is in the corridor she frees herself of them, fetches a pail of water, washes off her shoes and wipes the floor.

In her mind's eye she sees Max struggling to get up the embankment, slipping back with his fingers clutching bunches of grass, how awkwardly he gets up, while she, the idea takes hold of her, virtually stalked up like a chamois. What is so special about walking on the ties? He was a linesman and has two straight healthy legs! And after all, what is involved in walking on the ties? It's not difficult with two healthy feet. A mindless movement forwards, all in all; only leg-work and not brain-work.

Roswitha's hip hurts from the rapid walking. The really stressful part was the walk there, with no noonday rest beforehand. This Sunday she was on her legs much longer than Max, who took it easy; nevertheless she had to go behind him, to stop and pant; he showed no consideration. She thinks she held up well. Walking on ties, in and of itself, would be nothing special for her even in dry weather when she was well rested. Perhaps, though, she could be content in the future with climbing up railway embankments, she should perfect this skill.

She stands at the window, looks into the rain and waits for Leimer. The ploughed up landscape stretches out below her window. That doesn't make her happy. She goes into the kitchen, warms water to wash herself. She wants to change her clothes.

Finally everything is done, even the washbasin and stand stowed away. It is getting dark. On this cloudy late summer day dusk falls early, as if from one day to the next they had slid into a later season. Their evening mealtime is approaching.

Again she sits at the window. A feeling of coldness is rising from her feet. Later she gets up and prepares the meal. She sets the table; when she is already half the way to the window again she forces herself back and finishes preparing the food. Then she rushes to the window. She seeks reasons that might explain the long time he has been away: He couldn't stop going; he got intoxicated by the movement and lost all track of time and place. But perhaps he fell; although he had once been an experienced walker and, as she saw today, immediately became one again; she cannot entirely rule out that he might have stumbled on the slippery ties when he, already tired from the long walk, got inattentive and finally fell and couldn't go any farther, lay on the ties with broken bones or bruised ankles and the train came pounding along with its steam locomotive and ran over him. This was the time it had to come, the evening train. This was its doing.

She wants to steer her thoughts in another direction and thinks fleetingly about what else she could still do today. Prepare some things for tomorrow, some sewing work. Soak the laundry. But she doesn't move from the spot, although her feet are getting stiff from the cold and immobility and her back is numb. She has snuggled her cheek against her knee and put her arms around her legs. She keeps looking out the window, her gaze always fixed on the same spot, the elderberry bush where Max would have to become visible if he came.

Her parents had not come back. The fact that she had sat here thirty years ago and waited in vain with the same rigid fear is a sign for her. Everything will repeat itself, screams an inner voice, it is fate! Oh this traffic! The mail busses had brought about the disaster for her parents. Ever since then Roswitha has avoided them. She doesn't travel. The fatal outing had arisen from a whim of her father's, who had been promoted from mail bus driver to foreman in the mail bus repair workshop. Together with his wife, he wanted to travel the route one last time, as a passenger. For more than twenty years he had driven the route, sitting behind the steering wheel in the performance of his job. They had disappeared behind the elderberry bush. Roswitha, who had stayed home alone, had watched them go, but they hadn't turned around; they also hadn't come back that way again. Roswitha had sat silently at the window the whole night long. In the morning, instead of her parents, her sister and brother-in-law had emerged from behind the elderberry bush and come toward the house, and Roswitha – she was still almost a child then, fourteen years old – had screamed and raced down the stairs and out the door, because she had suddenly already known everything. Her sister's face had brought her the news of their deaths. The local newspapers had been full of the accident the next day. In a blind curve, a transport truck had come toward the mail bus, the driver had braked hard immediately, the brakes had locked, and the bus had broken through the guard rail and rolled over into the hazel bushes in the ditch. The driver and her parents, who contrary to regulations were standing at the front beside the driver, had been seriously injured and died on the way to the hospital. The other passengers, there had also been three older women and two young men in the bus, had gotten away with bruises. They later unanimously said in their statements to the police that Roswitha's father had entertained the whole bus with his jokes; the old women and the young men said they had seldom had such an amusing trip. Her father had told countless anecdotes from his time as a driver, and while doing so he put his arm around her mother, who interjected again and again that there wouldn't be any more such fun in the workshop. Things would be different there.

Roswitha had not known this happy father who could make people laugh. In the first years after his death, she had looked at his suits again and again, and in the beginning had also buried her face in the jackets which still held his smell. And she had felt the wide leather belt that he could pull out of the loops on his pants so skillfully it just made a rasping noise, and that he brought smacking down on her bottom when she had gone against his instructions, or her mother's or the catechist's or the teacher's. He did that because he loved her. He went to the trouble after a long stressful day at work to attend to his naughty daughter, to this rascal. Sometimes with impatience, sometimes with excitement she awaited the punishment that always came. When it was over and she ran her fingertips over the red welts, she had the feeling that order had been restored. Her father had taken care of her. Without saying a word, he let his blows rain down on her posterior (because she was a girl, she was allowed to keep her clothes on, he would have hit a son, her father said, on the bare ..., but he didn't have a son), the only sounds were the snapping of the leather when her father raised his arm, and his heavy breathing. His panting belonged to her. She belonged to her father, who was always right. Her mother had never really been visible behind her father. Roswitha had always related to her father. Her mother had never hit her. She can't stop mourning her father. Her mother has long since been dead. Sometimes she had gotten angry with her dead father because she had the feeling he had kept something from her. She had never known this joker. It occurs to her that since Max Leimer has entered her life she has almost forgotten her father. And that she has felt good about doing so. But now she is sitting at the window again as she had then, waiting and staring out and not moving, afraid to move, in case that would bring something into motion that she would not be able to handle. She acts calm, as if her fear and anguish were put in cold storage. In the hours she waits for Max, or rather no longer waits for him, she thinks only of the disaster that for her has already happened.

Meanwhile night has fallen and the elderberry bush has long since been swallowed by darkness; so she would no longer be able to see the man coming. But Roswitha doesn't move from the spot, as if there is a spell on her. Now that her eyes can no longer see anything in the black of night, she has closed them. Everything in her is listening. With her heightened expectation of hearing something, she would know the location of every tremor in the floorboards, every slight stirring and movement. She perceives the everyday sounds, this concert of whispering and tapping, crunching and knocking, in a way that makes her head whirl and her ears buzz, turning her into a trembling receiver with raised antennae.

At some point she hears him coming. His steps are audible all the way from the elderberry bush. She doesn't leap up, she remains in her entwined position, but her body awakes, it throbs and hammers; now his steps are splashing in the puddles. She tears herself out of her embrace and staggers to her feet, rubs her calf and shin that now have a prickling sensation. That is the life returning. Now everything hurts, and already his steps are thudding in the stairway. Hesitant steps, different. Or the steps of a stranger? Then she thinks: Or is he hurt? Now the key is turned in the lock. She touches her hairdo and stumbles to the light switch. Then he is already standing at the threshold and flings open the door so that it bangs against the wall. They blink at each other out of narrowed eyes, both blinded by the light. He sways a little and comes in with faltering steps in dirty shoes. Every step deposits a watery clump of earth on the floor. The man she has longed for staggers and grins at her, giving her a fright. He smells of the pub. She knows the smell from her father. She gets out of Max's way. Sluggishly, he tells her something about the pub and friends. He mentions names that Roswitha has never heard. They were there too, he says, and he threw with his knives and won. He beat everyone. He remained unbeaten. He lets himself fall onto the stool and is now sitting so low down that Roswitha can look down at him and imagine he is kneeling before her. No, it's certainly not that, she gives herself a mental smack on the mouth. Max has difficulty with his shoes. He wants to remove them, stepping with one foot against the heel of the other. Roswitha looks at the struggling man, then at the mud puddles on the linoleum, then at the man again, who is still panting and struggling unsuccessfully with his shoes. Boot-jack, he yells, bring the boot-jack, and yells louder and louder. Psst, says Roswitha. But no one can hear them. Then she kneels down in front of him and fiddles with his knotted shoelaces with her beautiful fingers and their round manicured nails. Max raises his upper body clumsily and leans back letting his head fall against the wall. Between half closed eyelids he stares at the bowed figure undoing his shoelaces.

He sits, his breath whistles softly. He grins incessantly. Roswitha watches her agile fingers unraveling the shoelaces, the knots are finally undone. She struggles with his shoes. He lets it happen as if it doesn't concern him. At last she squeezes the shoes, which are wet through and through and caked with mud, from his feet. Max starts to roar with laughter, gives the crouching woman a kick so that she tips to the side, and screams: boot-jack! Roswitha gets over it quickly, she knows he didn't mean it in anger, he is laughing and having fun; but she puts his shoes right into the washbasin, scrubs them clean and stuffs them with newsprint. Finally she wipes up the hall. Roswitha has newfound strength. Max is still sitting on his stool in the corner and watching her. Sometimes he sighs. Roswitha turns her head toward him over her cleaning rag: Is he sick, or does he want to say something? But he is silent. And it is good that he is here.

Finally, when she is finished with all the cleaning, she leaves him alone and retreats into her workshop. It is already past midnight and high time for her to get to sleep.

Roswitha turns down her sheets, slips into her nightgown, then the door opens and Max comes into her room without knocking. He has undressed and washed. His eyebrows are still shining with moisture and his hair is wet and smoothed straight back. He is wearing nothing but gray-blue underpants that are torn in several places. Roswitha is horrified: what is he thinking of, descending on me, as it were, with his hairy chest, his thighs, his calves? She looks quickly away from the torn underpants (the holes also remind her of her duty to darn them) and studies the red and black shepherd's plaid pattern of her slippers. I must take him to task for this, she thinks. But then his hands grab her shoulders, he smells of soap. Well, he says, and shoves his knee against her thigh, well. I must repel him, thinks Roswitha, a decent woman does not let herself be treated in this manner. She wants to be conquered, but first laid siege to, persistently, and then taken by storm. Roswitha would like to see everything be romantic. She longs for compliments, flattery, tenderness, and vows of love. She has heard and read of that, and seen it shown in films. Besides, there is a sentence in her sex education book: "No woman needs to be ashamed of her natural feelings, but she must guard against losing her self-control and sacrificing her dignity." Roswitha has elevated this sentence to a maxim for herself. Dignity, self-control, the uppermost women's virtues. No, today she would not give in to his courting, no matter how much he pleaded.

But Max isn't thinking of that at all. Come, he demands brusquely, shoving her again with his knee, this time in the rear end. Forward! Let's fuck, dummy! You're no young person any more.

Roswitha is at a loss as to how to react, so doesn't move from the spot. He lets go of her: Do you want to or don't you? To her own astonishment Roswitha hears herself whisper: Don't know. It's not proper. Then Max begins to laugh again uncontrollably, not proper, not proper, grabs her by the waist and pushes her through the corridor, through the dark hallway into the bedroom. Roswitha lets herself be pushed forward and thinks that she is thereby at least offering some resistance.

Don't make such a fuss, he pants, as she stands stiff as a poker in front of the bed. Lie down, he commands, damn it! Then she lies down obediently, because now she is afraid he might back off again, his plan seems suddenly so incidental, even bothersome to him. Yet she has read in her book and retained exactly that the sexual drive is of greatest importance above all for the man, and the man by nature is the courting, tackling and giving party. The woman, however, is the opposite.

Still don't know what to do, that can't be true, you're still a virgin? he asks. Roswitha blushes, but thank goodness he can't see that in the darkness. She is silent and lies on her back and puts both hands at her sides. Max slips off his underpants and throws himself beside her. A virgin, he says, an old maid, and again starts to laugh. Then he gets straight to the point and goes to work on her body in an experienced manner. Her nightgown is quickly shoved up, her underpants pulled from her hips, her thighs spread. Stay like that, he orders. She doesn't dare to move for fear of doing something wrong, and just trembles. Shame heats up her body like a fever: a virgin, untouched, at 42 years of age.

Then he kneels over her, brings his genitals into contact with her, Roswitha can't see that because all is black around her, because there is nothing at all to see, but then she feels something live hopping between her bravely spread legs, something not cold, not warm, not hard, not soft. He tilts her pelvis, adjusts her again, seeks her opening with his hands, widens it with his fingers, which hurts, and sticks a viscous blob of saliva on her vagina. Roswitha takes note of everything so that she can tell herself about it later. He doesn't give any more instructions; he consists only of hand gestures and loud breathing. Roswitha regards the breathing as a good sign, like the suitcase he brought when he came to her. She seems to be giving the man more trouble than reward, more pain than gain. It concerns her that it is so difficult for him, in spite of his circumspect preparations, to enter into her with his impressive erectile tissue. She makes an effort to keep her legs spread, and he hits against her centre like against a wall. Finally he takes hold of himself with his hand and shoves and rubs himself into her. The deflowering is painful, Roswitha has read. In any case it is unpleasant. And it takes a while. Nevertheless, she regards the movements of his body, the size and strength of his penis that now, as she feels, seems to fill the area of her stomach, and the panting and sweating of the man as her work. From her neck to her knees she has felt this man's skin like homage to her, this rough, slightly prickly skin, that later feels moist, and finally relaxes heavy and warm as his breathing calms down.

Now it is over. Max gets up on his knees and wipes off his genitals. Roswitha feels like crying. That too, she knows, is natural after the first time. She sits up, reaches for her underpants that are tangled at her ankles, pulls them up, climbs out of bed and sneaks from the room, unnoticed by Max, who has fallen asleep right away.

As she goes she feels a warm moistness between her legs that cools off on her underpants.

She is dead tired, but she still has to wash herself before she can go to bed. In the lavatory she mixes a warm, tender bubble bath for herself. With it she washes the foreign matter from her body. Then she puts the wash utensils back in their place.

In bed, she sobs awhile to herself. That calms her. Finally she falls asleep; and everything is as if nothing had happened.

A few hours later she wakes up with a start. She opens her eyes. Her fingers lie temptingly on the blanket like a spider's web.

So last night it happened. Roswitha relives it many times in the course of the day; whether she is leading the needle delicately through fine chiffon or whether she has the sewing machine clattering along a seam: again and again the event, broken up into separate pictures, moves past her inner eye. In the attempt to bring order into her thoughts, she tries to reduce what she has experienced to one result. She asks herself: What did I expect? How did I imagine the first time would be, and how was it really? All things considered, what did I get from it?

She often dreamed of it, earlier very often, when she was still younger, in recent times less often though, and right now it has happened. She must admit she is disillusioned. It was like being at the gynecologist's. Before it happened, her hands were a little sweaty with excitement and she felt the urge to urinate, and afterwards, a modest sense of satisfaction that it was over. But now she is also somewhat proud. A man has desired her, she aroused him, he was really keen on her. That is new; she had become an object of desire, of longing. He desired, it transpired, occurs to her, and she laughs quietly because it rhymes. I can provide, but he may also be denied. Another rhyme. I am a woman and have a power, she thinks, since last night. There is nothing about that in the sex education books. My female body has proved its worth. Now I am relieved. I feel I have been put into service. I like it when everything in me and around me is functioning.

Otherwise nothing has changed between them. He doesn't say anything at breakfast, is silent and dull, interested only in the coffee and bread, and doesn't refer to the occurrence of the night with as much as the batting of an eyelid. But after breakfast, when he is gone, Roswitha is drawn to his bed in the bedroom. And lo and behold, it is the first time it hasn't been made. The pillow and quilt are crumpled on the mattress, the sheet is shockingly displaced. And she is dutiful and plumps up the quilt and cushion, pulls the sheet taut again and is – strangely enough – contented. He laid his hands on her, she lays her hands on his bed, and in this manner they are obliged to each other, quasi hand in hand, their hands are laid in each other. Engaged, she whispers and smiles astonished and pleased with her own deep thoughts. Then she takes a second sheet and makes the bed beside his.

In the afternoon Lotte appears again unexpectedly. She is bringing Roswitha a written invitation to the first preliminary meeting of the stage production on the coming Wednesday in the parish hall. Lotte will pick her up.

Lotte is in a great hurry again, but she verbosely urges her friend to come to the meeting. Roswitha belongs with people. She lives too secluded a life, Lotte thinks. Roswitha smiles and thinks her hour has come. She confesses that for a few days now she has not been alone at all any more. Lotte says: Well I am speechless. She is suddenly no longer happy, but rather put out, and only says that she would like to know everything in detail and who and from where, and that Roswitha is a still water, and actually she is a little insulted by so much secretiveness, and that she is always available to talk and help out and unfortunately has no more time now and that Roswitha should make sure it doesn't cost her money. And whoosh, Lotte is out of the apartment and out of the building.

    She let the invitation flutter down on the parish librarian's dirndl. Miss Greta has gone on a diet and now needs to have the seams taken in. Roswitha takes the dirndl dress with the red top and the black velvet braid trimmings and puts it on the tailor's dummy. Then she reads the piece of paper. She doesn't understand what she is supposed to do at such a "meeting," but the invitation is obviously connected with her pledge of support.

    Later she sees Max slaving away below her sewing room. Then she forgets about the theater and culture and watches him work for a while. He is piling boards on top of each other again, has no helper and is audibly struggling. His panting can be heard all the way up to her apartment. Then she steps back from the window, sits down and places her hands in each other. She still hears him working, breathing loudly, and shoving and rubbing the boards against each other. She moves her chair closer again to the window, surreptitiously watches the panting worker, at the same time presses the palms of her hands against her mouth, draws her fingers individually over her incisors, licks them and bites her knuckle joints. Later she puts three little Band-Aids on the tiny wounds so that no drop of blood can fall on her sewing; she gets to work on Miss Greta's dirndl, sits at the sewing machine with it and takes in the seams. Then she pulls it over the tailor's dummy again, closes the buttons and the hooks, sees that it fits, and is satisfied. In the meantime Max has also finished with his work. It's time to stop work for the day.

    Today he comes on time for the evening meal. Everything's going like clockwork. The wash table stands ready in the hall. In the kitchen the table is set. She tells him about Lotte, who has invited her to a meeting about a planned stage production. He repeats "stage production," in his mouth it sounds like an expression from a foreign language. That's nothing for me he says at last, I'd rather do kniving. Roswitha asks what that is, "kniving." It's a word he made up for his knife-throwing. She asks if he would show her the kniving, she can't picture what it is. Yes indeed, says Max and goes into the bedroom. Roswitha feels her heart pounding and says to herself: I am probably happy now.

In the bedroom he sees that the bed beside his is made with matching sheets with little flowers. He stands still awhile before the wall where the colorful picture of the heart pierced with seven swords is hanging. The heart is fiery red, the seven swords stick into the heart up to the hilt and their points protrude on the other end. The points are bluish. Yellow flames are licking between the two rounded upper edges of the heart. Beneath the heart, two hands hold a lily whose white blooms unfold above the little fire. There is no face to be seen in the picture. That's strange, but not funny. Max pulls five smaller flick knives out of the loops of his knife chest, tests their mechanism, looks around in the room, observes the picture, the brass bars on the bed, the sheets on the second bed, and then he does find it funny, he bursts out laughing and can't regain his composure, and brays and doubles up. Roswitha comes in when she hears the noise. She doesn't know what to think of the laughter. Max's face is bluish-red and contorted. He has thrown himself on the bed and is kicking his legs. Has he gone crazy, thinks Roswitha, or does he have St. Vitus's dance? Or is he just amused? In that case she could also laugh. And she tries to. Max pauses to catch his breath and wipes the tears from his eyes; he sees Roswitha standing there and immediately begins to laugh again, punching her with his fists. That may be still a joke, thinks Roswitha, but it hurts, and she tries to evade his boxing blows. Then he turns into a hunter, he leaps up and teases her with his fists, now joking, now really poking. But now Roswitha has had enough, and she is also afraid of his wide open mouth with his fleshy tongue rolling in it. She wants to go back to the kitchen, maybe out of the house. Max, however, wants to play around with her, so it seems she is a spoilsport, he pushes her through the room toward the bed, and now she is lying there. Don't! she screams. Then he throws himself over her. I am defenseless, Roswitha says to herself. He bores his elbow against her shoulder and pushes her into the pillow, the other hand reaches under her dress. How agilely he frees himself, and how quickly he pushes his penis into her! Yesterday's awkward fellow has become a master. Roswitha, of course, does not appreciate that. Her pelvis is the dance floor on which he is doing the Schuhplattler.[1] None of this is in her sex education book. During the activity some of the little Band-Aids on the back of her hand come loose, and blood is dripping out of the small wounds. She sucks on the bleeding parts, sucks her sobbing over the backs of her hands. And a short distance over her she sees Leimer's red face, his mouth terribly twisted, his panting has become raspy, and his pulled back lips reveal his rotten teeth. He unloads himself quickly. There is something thrilling about that. But unfortunately everything in her is hurting. Everything? Everything. Everything. Then he falls beside her and is gentle as a lamb for a moment. But she wants to cry. She stays lying down and sobs loudly; he should hear it, because he should comfort her. Max moves, gets up muttering, puts on his pants and goes into the kitchen. Roswitha hears him lighting a cigarette and then inhaling deeply. Her tears stick in her throat, she sneaks back to her workshop through the corridor and thinks that maybe she should start smoking too. Meanwhile it is getting dark. She goes to the open window. It already smells of autumn. The barred windows of the prison wing cling blackly to the floodlit facade. Two guards with shouldered arms patrol behind the barbed wire fence. They amble, one in this direction, one in the other, turn around and come back toward each other again. Halfway along the lengthy prison wing stands a narrow guard's hut that resembles an old-fashioned telephone booth. When the guards reach it, they turn around and walk back the same stretch. When the weather is bad, they take turns staying in the hut.

Previously, before there was a barbed wire fence along the prison, individual inmates succeeded again and again in escaping, in spite of the guards. People heard and read of daredevil undertakings, of sheets woven into ropes, of sawed through bars, of fugitives who swam across the river in order to make their way farther on the other side, provided with clothes by accomplices. They usually didn't get far. Almost everyone who escaped was

---

[1] The Schuhplattler is a Bavarian folkdance involving slapping of the thighs, knees, and shoe soles.

picked up again within a few days. Some even came back of their own accord.

The high barbed wire fence and the observant human surveillance prevent anyone from escaping these days. Roswitha sighs, because Max crosses her mind again, and everything else. She stands at the window and watches the men silently going back and forth, and always in the reddish yellow light of the floodlight. Everything is quiet. The quiet seems to spread out from the black squares of the windows. Even the rushing of the river seems to her today like a quiet murmuring. And she calms herself. Are the watchmen not also keeping watch for her? They protect the freedom of the free and watch over the confinement of the convicts. Roswitha is proud of this thought. She would like to have shared it with someone before she forgot it again. Strange, she thinks, now of all times, and why did I not think this deep thought until today, given that I'm more than used to the prison, it's a part of my life like the parish garden, like the church and like the convicts. The order, the routine, the predictability comfort me, she realizes. So much in her life is in commotion, but the church and the prison, the barbed wire and the patrolling guards seem made for eternity. They remain. Almost every day when Roswitha goes shopping, she meets smaller or larger groups of prisoners in gray, on their way in step accompanied by guards. Until now she has hardly paid attention to them. No face has remained in her memory. The only distinguishing feature, which seems to erase every personal characteristic, is the dark gray, coarse clothing with the big black letter "P" on the jacket. P for prison.

People who must know, including Lotte, whose husband is a prison guard, say that the inmates have too good a life in prison. It's almost a resort. There are more than a few of them who do something crooked almost as soon as they are released, just to get put in prison again. There they are fed, have a bed and a roof over their heads. Nothing is lacking in the prison except, naturally, freedom. But, like everything, one can give up freedom.

The best proof of that was the star of the institution, the serial rapist-murderer who had killed three women with a hammer, including a nurse who had a relationship with the head physician and was pregnant by him, which was only revealed by the autopsy, and who after serving his lifetime sentence, which is fifteen years here, refused to leave the institution. Freedom frightened him. That was enough to get him transferred from the prison to the lunatic asylum in the capital city. He longed to get back to his cell though.

That speaks for the pleasant conditions in the prison. Because of that, Roswitha can stand at the window with a deep feeling of well-being, looking sometimes at the wing with the detention cells and the guards, and other times at the more brightly illuminated church with its verdigris onion towers. Architecturally, the church and the prison are not separated. Only an internal wall separates the place of worship from the place of punishment.

She is tired, but also relaxed. She goes into the bedroom. Max doesn't move any more. He is already sleeping deeply. Without turning on the light, she slips to his side, in order to sleep beside him for the first time. That has come faster than she had thought. Today she even forgets to wash herself. That occurs to her later, and she is a little startled. But then she is already half asleep. At some time in the night she wakes up. Max is snoring.

Now they have also put scaffolding along the side where her workshop is. Only the bedroom side remains undisturbed. She flees to it to get away from the noise and dirt. During the day she can't open any of the windows any more. On three sides of the house they are knocking the plaster off. The dust coats the windowpanes, which have become almost opaque. The fine particles come through all the cracks, Roswitha thinks she can even hear the dust crunching between her teeth. The work and the surrounding devastation have made her nervous. Sewing is no longer easy. There is dust everywhere; no matter what she takes hold of, the dust crumbles and crunches everywhere, between her hands, under her fingernails, on her fingertips; the smooth metal of the sewing machine has to be wiped off again and again. And a gray film on the furniture, on the linoleum. At times she thinks she feels her entire body shrouded in a scratching outer skin. At lunchtime she asks Max how long that's going to go on. She is already losing her appetite. She thinks she is biting on sand between the dumplings. The knocked off stucco seems to want to distribute itself on the salad and the meat. Doesn't he, Max, notice anything? Does nothing bother him? Max shakes his head and declares that women are all hysterical and oversensitive. It will pass. In one, two weeks all the old plaster will be off and then they can start putting on the new. Max has to go to his work again.

Roswitha doesn't sneak to the window to watch him anymore. She doesn't want to perceive anything more of the outside. Now she seeks refuge in the bedroom. After lunch she lies on the bed here, enjoying the quiet, because the hammering sounds as if it is coming from far away, the river drowns out everything, it lulls her to sleep. She dreams of a bathtub full of warm water and a perfumed bubble bath in it. When he moved in, Max had promised her a bath. Yes indeed, it will be done, he had maintained. But until now he has made no further mention of it. She longs so much to lie in water, to use soap extravagantly, in order finally to get rid of this scratching on her skin. She curses the awkward and involved procedure of getting washed by splashing water on herself. Previously she went to her sister's regularly to take a bath. That practice was discontinued a few years ago, without Roswitha being able to remember what the reason had been.

Even the sky is dusty gray; Roswitha is suffering from the sultriness. If only the storm would finally break! This build-up of clouds and dust! It's suffocating.

On the way to Martha's, on the street lined with chestnut trees, she meets Lotte's husband with a group of prisoners. She casts a brief glance at the convicts. They are, in fact, faceless. The coarse dark gray clothing has stripped them of their faces. The guard, by way of contrast, looks handsome in his uniform. It is the uniform that gives him a face. Roswitha has occasionally seen Hermann Spannring in civilian clothes. The regulation cap conceals his smooth bald head. Without his official hat his face looks bloated. But as soon as he puts on the cap with the dark green peak and the gold braid, his features become tauter, his eyes shine, and probably because as an official he always holds up his chin – which is now looking bombastically broad – his lips become visible as a narrow line. Indeed, he is a handsome man when he is marching beside the gray figures and raises his hand to his cap to greet Roswitha. How good Leimer would look in uniform, even in civilian clothes he would look better than Lotte's husband. Did he wear a uniform when he was a linesman? She will have to ask him sometime. Everything fits so tightly on people in uniform. And these perfectly pressed creases in the black gabardine pants; they lend the men's steps an imperious grace. Roswitha is surprised at what she is noticing today and formulating in words. Previously I never noticed things like that; or did I simply not think about them? Or were men never that much in my thoughts before? But now that I have one, do I think I have acquired a right to all of them?

Martha acts pleased to see her sister unexpectedly. Roswitha is very relieved. Martha – who of course has always been moody – is on an even keel again. This is how she is on good days. Bruno sticks his head in through the living room door, which is slightly ajar. He is sick, explains Martha. What's wrong with you? Roswitha asks. His stomach is bothering him again, her sister answers, the same old story. Could you make me another cup of chamomile tea? He turns to his wife. As hot as possible. Bruno withdraws again.

Martha goes into the kitchen to get the chamomile tea. Before doing so, she invites Roswitha to take a bath right away without standing on ceremony, she knows the custom.

While the water is running in the tub, Roswitha slips out of her clothes. She trickles fragrant bath-salts into the stream of water. The mirror over the washbasin shows her naked upper body. The skinny breasts displease her. Loose hanging sacks of skin over her ribs. Pathetic. And nipples like dried plums. The bra corrects a lot. The water rushes and rises and steams at her back as she climbs onto the edge of the tub to get away from the breasts to her hips and thighs. I'm crazy, she says to herself as she clambers about dangerously on the smooth narrow edge. At last she has her navel and belly in the mirror. She makes a circular motion with her pelvis. That pleases her better. The curve of her hips makes her think of a vase. But she is embarrassed again by her hairy private parts, as if they belonged to someone else, and as if it were tactless to gape at them. As if caught at it, she covers the place between her legs with her hand. With her other hand she has to steady herself against the wall. My beautiful hand as a fig leaf, she thinks. But that's enough now. What has Max seen of her body? Nothing clearly, only indistinctly, she suspects. Quickly she glides into the tub, splashes around in the water and in no time is wrapped in a fragrant cloak of bubbles. Roswitha sighs with sheer contentment. Then there is a knock at the door. Martha wants to come in. Roswitha would rather have been alone. Now she remembers why she stopped coming to Martha's to take a bath. Her sister never let her bathe without disturbing her. She always wanted to come in, usually just when Roswitha was lying naked in the tub or was just about to get out. I could tell her she should stay out, Roswitha thinks for a moment. But that would have seemed impertinent to her. Does she have a right to be here undisturbed? Her sister has already come in, Roswitha slides down to her neck under the carpet of foam. It is always unspeakably embarrassing for her to show herself naked in front of her sister.

Martha pulls a stool into the narrow space alongside the tub. Now I'm caught, thinks Roswitha. I can't get out of the water without stepping on my sister. Martha fiddles with her apron-strings and looks darkly at the bubbly surface. My God, she's in a bad mood again, thinks Roswitha. I shouldn't have come. Then Martha starts to talk. It's all confused. Roswitha doesn't understand anything. Martha is prattling away and staring at her apron-strings as she toys with them. It all sounds so crazy. Bruno has another woman, and she herself has breast cancer. Roswitha doesn't believe a word of what her sister is saying, she is now plucking at her apron-strings with dogged determination and not looking up and mixing up what she is saying, about an operation and about men, who are all the same, and that Bruno was being unfaithful to her with a hussy, a witch, she knew who she was, a really cunning one, she knew the so-and-so exactly, and they were going to cut off one of her own breasts, one or even both, and then as a woman she was on the trash heap anyway. Then Martha laughs the way she laughed back when Roswitha told her of her forthcoming marriage, and now Roswitha is almost convinced that her sister has cracked up, and thinks to herself, the best thing is to say nothing and just act as if I believe everything, I'll nod and roll my eyes sympathetically or something like that. What else should I do? Roswitha is starting to shiver beneath her cushion of bubbles. Either Martha will go at last, so that she can climb out of the tub, or she will have to run more hot water. Martha is silent, but stays sitting down. Roswitha turns on the warm water tap. That gives Martha a fright. At last she stands up, looks at Roswitha for the first time since she came in and utters threats. Against me? Roswitha asks herself, or does she mean Bruno and the other woman? Then Martha puts her finger on her mouth and says, psst, not a word, psst. And goes. Roswitha crawls shivering out of the tub, dries herself. She remembers that Martha was always particularly strange when it was full moon. Surely she won't go crazy. Is it menopause?

When Roswitha wants to say good-bye to her sister, her brother-in-law informs her through the glass door of the living room that his wife has gone shopping in the meantime. Roswitha hurries home depressed. It's time for the evening meal. As she enters the house --the construction site is already abandoned -- the first drops of a short but violent thunder shower are falling.

Roswitha lies alone in the double bed and is afraid. It must be almost midnight already, and still they are making a noise. Sometimes she can make out Max's laugh and his loud talking.

Her father brought company home sometimes too. Colleagues from work. Her mother always had to be prepared for that. As far as Roswitha can remember, she never protested. Only in the kitchen had she groaned and let herself fall on the chair and wrung her hands. But soon afterwards she was ready and smiled at the men, bringing them beer or fruit wine, bacon and bread. Her father had insisted that such supplies always be in the house.

Her father's friends had been loud too, had laughed, later shouted and also argued. She had been afraid then too, with her father behaving so differently among his friends, he didn't seem to know her anymore, not even to see her, he belonged to the men, she was forgotten. She also couldn't go to bed as long as the men were there, because they were sitting in her bedroom. Sometimes she was so tired she nodded off on the stool in the kitchen and awoke in her own bed. But opening her eyes had always been distressing for her because no one had cleared away the remains of the food and drink. Only after she woke up did the empty and half empty beer glasses on the table and the full ashtrays start to stink. The table was crooked, the chairs as if they had staggered there, the table cloth half pulled down on the divan. She dreaded getting up. The fact that her mother had not yet tidied up made Roswitha feel bitter toward her. Of course she knew that her mother would straighten and clean everything in the course of the day – that was comforting, to be sure –, but the moment was bleak. Her world was destroyed; it didn't console Roswitha that it would be repaired again, because she couldn't defend herself against its being destroyed again. Her security became a pseudo security, something borrowed. Roswitha had thought she had been able to forget her childhood fears. Now they are rising up in her again. Sometimes, on the morning after such late night parties, her father had been gentle and good-natured. He tugged at her braids for fun or he noticed something about her clothing, in short, she was there again for him. That made things much better.

It occurs to her that she should not have let the men into her apartment and at the same time, that she would never have the courage to turn them away. It is this insight too that is keeping her awake, not just the howling and the blaring of the accordion. She would not be able to refuse her future husband the company of his friends. She would not be able to prevent their drinking here or Max's playing with his knives with them. She hears the hard clang of the knives hitting on the pastry board – she had even provided them with that.

Max doesn't need to have Roswitha offer them food and drink. She had just had to make room for him on the table where her sewing things lay. Then he sent her to bed. Now she is lying there and waiting, for what? For sleep, for Max? For many things. She looks at her hands. Moonlight is shining through the light curtains. She raises her arms and bends her fingers, one after the other. Then they look like black claws. That makes her sob. She dreads that, like she dreads vomit. Later her crying sinks into a whimper. That sounds mournful, and her own voice frightens her. They stop playing the accordion. There is clattering and crashing about in her apartment. Roswitha hopes they are leaving. Maybe Max will soon come to her and will still see or hear that she is crying. And will console her. Just the thought of that dries her tears. She feels her heart beating wildly; it seems to her that she is happy. She listens. Footsteps, the opening and shutting of the door, sudden brief laughter, talking; without a doubt, the men are breaking up. Roswitha lies stiff with suspense. Max will have to come. Where else should he go? She is giving him a place to stay and quarters. Then she senses a dark feeling spread through her body like heat, she is angry. That makes her ready to rebel. Ready to make reproaches and threats. Yes indeed. Capable of demanding a definite decision one way or the other. Humility and leniency are rejected. She sees the knives shimmering in the chest. Max has only taken out the top row of knives for his game, the ones with the smallest or finest blades. The rest of them throw shadows like incredibly long daggers. That comes from the particular way they are held in. The stabbing weapons jut out of a pointed corner of the opened container through a holder that Max himself designed and made, he has drawn her attention to it. Roswitha is straining her ears to hear if he is finally coming. She thinks of Martha's hands again, and how she wrapped the apron-strings around her fingers so tightly that her fingertips went blue. And Bruno's voice from the living room sounds suddenly in her ears. Martha had always been physically fit as a fiddle. Roswitha slips her hands under her nightgown and feels her breasts. Was it true that Bruno had another woman, or was Martha just imagining it? Roswitha regrets not having enquired. Is it someone from the village? – Then she hears footsteps in the kitchen, the floor creaks, chair legs scrape over the linoleum. Wasn't that the sound of a glass clinking? On and in her breasts there is nothing to discover. Why doesn't Martha want to tell her husband? Am I obliged to be silent because I didn't protest against her psst? Roswitha asks herself. That rubs her the wrong way. She would only too willingly have hung her sister's illness around Bruno's neck like a goiter. Martha is just imagining the illness. The hard lumps in her breast come and go. Bruno might say she was just trying to make herself interesting with it. People often say that of each other. Roswitha's father used to browbeat her the same way. When she had a toothache or a headache, or when she couldn't walk any farther because her hip hurt. Her father said she got aches and illnesses above all to make herself interesting. Then he deliberately avoided looking at her, to cure her of it. Her mother helped her secretly. But that didn't count.

Max still hasn't come. Some time ago the door to the lavatory squeaked on its hinges. What is he doing so long? Roswitha is impatient. The intense rage that made her come to life threatens to be worn down by the waiting. Already she discovers in herself a readiness to be reconciled, and she listens intently for sounds from the apartment. It's an effort for her to stay in bed. What is the meaning of this clattering, this constant opening and shutting of the door, this pushing and shoving? Is he moving cupboards, boxes at this late night, actually early morning, hour? And he doesn't come. Then it is quiet again outside. She stays where she is and doesn't know what to do. But then he is there! Suddenly the door opens, and he is there. He sneaks in. On his tiptoes and with his back hunched, but unsteady on his feet. Roswitha moves. He arrives humbly, that disarms her. The fact that he is making an effort to sneak in so considerately indicates that he is ashamed. He is indeed sorry for everything; she doesn't need to reproach him for anything any more. He has arrived at this insight on his own. Roswitha holds her breath. What will happen? He throws his cover back and crawls into bed. Quickly, he wraps himself up in the quilt so that Roswitha has only the slightest hint of a shock of his hair and a little bit of the back of his head beside her. He has immediately turned his back to her, and he seems to have fallen asleep at once. That speaks against a bad conscience. His breathing is deep and even at first, then it gets louder, grinding and snoring now short now long, now loud and now quiet. Since Roswitha is now prevented, once for all, from getting to sleep, her rage returns; also because he is showing her nothing but his back. She plucks at his quilt. Waits. His snoring is like big paw; she is shaken about by it.

She can't think any more. Just twitch from the droning of his sleep. And tear at his quilt until his back side is finally free before her. She hits it now with her fists. But right away she is tearing at his hair, pulling his ears and digging her fingernails into his cheek. Roswitha has never felt so alive. Finally the snoring stops. She bites his neck and thinks she tastes his blood. He wakes up with a start and begins to curse terribly. Their rage brings them together. He hits her in the face. She understands that. He is once again the more powerful one. And hits her violently. And takes her out of the quilt and wants to mount her. The stupid nightgown is in the way and spreads out and obstructs him and finally rips. That's how it has to be, thinks Roswitha, so that he is right on top of me and I feel his wooly chest hair on me and he squeezes and crushes and kneads me. And quick to learn, she opens her legs toward him. But nothing plunges in; there is just some pressing and pushing. That is all. It's like wadding wiping between her legs. But he is snorting in her face, she also puts up with some spit on his breath. And is full of passion. And yearning. And screams, maybe ox or bull or hop on, or youbullbullbullyou, ox. Then he takes the matter in hand. It is a pathetic little willy that he squeezes determinedly between her legs. Where is the straight tower, the horny one? Roswitha doesn't understand. What is she doing wrong? The man doesn't give up very quickly, neither does the woman. They rub and rage against each other and crave coitus. Roswitha rakes her fingernails over his back and upper arms, leaving red tracks. They roar at each other and take it as a caress. It is all in vain. Finally, tired out, they separate from each other. Roswitha falls asleep right away.

Roswitha gets up too late, so Max has to leave the house without breakfast. He works with an empty stomach on the outside of her workshop. She clearly recognizes his voice as she bends over to wipe the floor. Instead of doing her sewing, she first has to clean her workshop. She drags the table and chairs into the corridor, carries the glasses into the kitchen and collects the knives the men had been throwing around. They had used the big round pastry board from her kitchen as a target and drawn numbers and spirals on it with red tailor's chalk. The board has to be brushed off with hot water and the floor washed with soapsuds. There is beer sticking to it, and cigarette ashes, and someone had vomited on the way to the lavatory. Roswitha attends first of all to the articles of clothing belonging to her customers, which she had put in the cupboard to be on the safe side. Thank heavens they weren't damaged. They had also left the tailor's dummy alone, which they had pushed into the corner, with Miss Greta's dirndl dress. But they had rummaged through her threads, and the big scissors for cutting out material are stuck open in the linoleum. As she crouches on her knees and scrubs the floor and pulls the scissors out of the floor, she is puffing with indignation at Max, more so at his so-called friends. What a mess! The filthy pigs! Dirty riff-raff! Miserable rabble, the whole lot of them. She is letting off steam. Never again would she allow such a thing. Of course she didn't allow it this time either. She wasn't asked. She was simply overrun, to be precise. That's enough of that now and that's that and never ever again! Otherwise she would chase Max away. Yes, she would throw him out. She would have the power and the right to do so.

But now, how is she supposed to get all her work done this morning? Where, in this devastation, can she find the time for shopping and cooking? Roswitha is sliding under the window on all fours to polish the linoleum dry when she hears Max's voice. She doesn't understand the words, but the tone has acquired something boastful, rebellious. Max is shooting his mouth off to his fellow workers. That's new to her.

Suddenly she runs into shoes with her floor cloth. Roswitha is startled. Lotte is standing in front of her. Roswitha hadn't heard the doorbell, the door had been unlocked, so she had simply dared to come in, Lotte explains. As her friend is wondering what Roswitha is doing here, it looks like a thorough cleaning day, Roswitha knows right away how to explain it. She can no longer stand the dust, the dirt. And the fine materials that she has to work with might possibly suffer damage. That's why she had decided to do a major cleaning. Lotte wants to tell Roswitha something important. She helps her friend arrange the room. The table is back where it belongs, and the chairs are also quickly back in place. Roswitha thinks anxiously of the many glasses and empty beer bottles she has put in the kitchen. By no means should her visitor see the remains of a wild party. So they sit at the table in the sewing workshop. Lotte thinks Roswitha has reason to celebrate. She winces inwardly and thinks her friend has seen through her. But Lotte is talking about something else. Something significant is in the works for Roswitha. Lotte is showing off again with the historical drama and the 1000-year jubilee and the school inspector who is a genuine poet and who has asked her, Lotte, to ask Roswitha if she wants to sew the historical costumes for the medieval drama. Of course I want to, Roswitha answers, feeling flattered, but also caught unawares; but whether I can? Lotte convinces Roswitha that she can do it, that she is the only one they considered capable of fitting out the pages, knights and ladies.

Lotte has left Roswitha beside herself with excitement. Your name will be on the playbills, she hears Lotte saying. Costumes: Roswitha Mantler. Of course she continues with her cleaning, washes the glasses and unravels the threads, but while doing so she is constantly thinking of the costumes she will be able to sew, probably even design. She would wallow in materials and ideas. Finally she would have the opportunity to demonstrate her skill. Alterations would have to wait and get shoved to the side. She has shoved Max to the side as well, who at noon wants to have his meal as he has in the meantime become accustomed to having it. He finds nothing but the flustered Roswitha who – again obsequious and feeling guilty – in great haste cooks a thick soup with sausages cut into it. She doesn't think of herself; she is still so excited that she can't eat anything. Meanwhile, Max washes himself. Roswitha recognizes that she has neglected him. Now she has nothing more to reproach him for. Roswitha works out the bill: they are even with each other. She is relieved about that. When the brown soup and the bread are on the table, she thinks about next Wednesday, when she is supposed to be present at a meeting for the first time. She would receive a personal letter from the school inspector. Lotte has announced it, Lotte, who has the lead role in the play, a damsel of the castle who fears for the life of her beloved knight.

Roswitha wants to make her ideas about the costumes clear at the first meeting. She is taking on an important task that will bring her into the public eye. In the afternoons she searches in her encyclopedia "The World from A to Z" for historical costumes, for ideas to fire her imagination.

So he is going by himself, Roswitha determines, he doesn't even ask me any more if I want to accompany him; he eats, drinks, washes himself, sleeps and comes and goes. She has run to the window to watch him go. His back has calmed her again. The piles of cement and gravel, the bushelbaskets and bricklayers' trowels lie around as if they wanted to stay here forever. Roswitha has become accustomed to them, just as she has become accustomed to the back of the man who just disappeared behind the elderberry bush.

No rain today, a warm Indian summer day in tired light. Max would have a nice walk on the ties. Maybe he would have uplifting thoughts if, while walking along the tracks, surrounded by late greenery, delighted by the branches trembling in the light, he would look up, look around him and finally become aware of the beauty of nature. Maybe he would want to talk when he returned. Roswitha is prepared to hope for everything. She is in a secure position because her apartment is clean again and the usual and necessary order has been restored in her workshop. Max and his friends have left no lasting traces.

Again she leafs through her only encyclopedia. She finds the keyword "Middle Ages." She looks for references to clothing customs and instructions. What did an unmarried noblewoman wear, what did a minnesinger? Roswitha has only vague ideas about it. Actually, she has urgent need of a picture book in which she would find medieval clothing depicted without all too much text. Unfortunately, the Middle Ages are dealt with in her reference work in a single meager sentence: "Middle Ages," she reads, "abbr. MA, designation for the period approx. from the decline of the Western Roman Empire (476), usually from roughly 500 A.D. to the discovery of the Americas (1492)."

That's of no use to her. A sentence in which nothing moves, no pictures rise up from it, she reads it and has already forgotten it. She isn't interested in the when and the where; she is looking for the how! How were the Middle Ages, abbreviated MA. How did people live, how did they dress; that above all is what Roswitha is eager to find out. She needs to know this for the first meeting. She has made up her mind about that. She wants to set her own ideas cautiously against the others' suggestions. In doing so, she wants to identify herself as an expert. Roswitha searches her memory. What does she know, what has she ever learned about the Middle Ages? She regrets her father's dislike of books. Other than the mentioned encyclopedia and a cookbook, her father had not allowed a book in the house. He himself set a good example and read nothing but the local newspaper. Lotte, who had books of fairytales and legends and also some girls' novels, encouraged Roswitha to read. She remembers: "The Most Beautiful Legends of the Middle Ages" were thrilling reading. She had read them secretly. For days she had been transformed. She had slipped into knights' suits of armor, had sat and fought on horseback. Siegfried, she calls out, Kriemhild and Gunther, and that scoundrel Hagen. Attila and the Huns, Dietrich of Bern. That's it, the Middle Ages. She can see it again. She recalls the colored illustrations in the book. The women, it rises up from her memory, wear long flowing robes, the sleeves come down to the wrists, beneath the bust a belt adorns the dress. Only Brunhild, the envious one, the traitor, has dark gathered hair. The knights came in armor. How should suits of armor be made? That's a headache for Roswitha. The parts of the armor could be formed out of cardboard and painted to have a metallic shine. But perhaps no armor would be necessary. After all, she didn't know the play yet. Maybe the actors would only be portraying unmarried noblewomen, pages and minnesingers. Maybe everything would take place inside a castle, with battles just being reported. Roswitha sees no difficulties in designing or sewing the pages' clothing. Tights would be suitable for the close-fitting pants. They can be bought. The rest, the tunics, are likewise easy to make, with the color co-ordination being the most challenging part.

Roswitha pushes a comfortable chair for herself onto the small spot of sun on the floor by the open window and looks through the boards and bars of the scaffolding to the prison across the way. Everything is peaceful. Again it is a comfort to her to watch the patrolling guards with their monotonous movements. In the prison, the former Benedictine monastery, Roswitha now sees a medieval castle: She sees noblewomen, pages and minnesingers walking about, Isolde of the White Hands waves a white handkerchief from a barred window. Roswitha falls asleep in the warm sunlight.

So he has come home drunk again, Roswitha determines as she prepares breakfast for him. She does not want to have to get used to his being drunk; she will make that clear to Max once and for all. Of course this time she didn't wait for him until she went numb like last week, but in the hours of being alone she did feel anger and bitterness. She sat alone at the table and ate the evening meal alone. Maybe it was the sight of the untouched place setting that let her feel such intense displeasure.

Later, when she was sitting in her sewing room again and thinking about the medieval heroic sagas and sinking deeper and deeper into her imagination – she saw tournaments, yearning minnesingers, King Arthur and the Knights of the Round Table, noblewómen – she forgot that she was waiting and forgot Max. She went to bed later than usual, around 11 o'clock. The empty bed at her side worried her a little. Soon she was asleep.

She dreamed she was being crushed under a steam roller. She screamed and woke up. Max was lying on top of her, and that explained the nightmare. Still, she couldn't breathe a sigh of relief. In the darkness over his shaded face she saw the crossbars of the window thrown blackly against the ceiling by the moonlight. Max had gone to work on the sleeping woman, already done a good job and cleared the way for himself. That it didn't occur to her to scream! Because I remained quiet, he didn't take my rejection seriously, she thinks now. Why didn't I implore him, distract him, even threaten him? Why didn't I let out piercing screams to intimidate him? He probably thought it was a game when I was hammering against his shoulders with my fists, she thinks and is appalled. We were panting at each other as if we were raging mad. We had already done that once before? Only clear words and screams for help would still have helped, she tells herself now. The misunderstanding is my fault. And now I'm making coffee and buttering bread for him. If only he hadn't stunk so much. He doesn't wash enough, not thoroughly enough, she determined again. With his body he pressed a smoky pub, urinal and bad liquor into hers. He let his impressive, but unwashed penis dance on her pubic hair. He could take the liberty of doing so, the gate was opened. I just let him do it, she remembers. But then I dug my fingernails into his back, yes, I even bit him hard in the shoulder. But that was really wrong, he took it differently, probably as a variety of love play. One mistake led to another. Then he grabbed my hands and squeezed them in his. I turned myself in the screw clamp. The only clever thing I did was to get quiet and submissive.

Roswitha puts the full coffee pot on the table and suddenly thinks: I could poison him. Or drug him. At least drug him.

I lay down for him the right way. I wriggled toward him with my vagina, for that I got my hands free when he had impaled me on his erectile tissue; that made up for its recent failure to perform. But that was bad for her. Roswitha, nothing but modeling clay beneath his virility, had not enjoyed it at all. She was worried about her fingers, in his fists the small joints had cracked.

That's how children are made, I thought, when he was finished. She didn't refer that to herself, she didn't need to fear or expect that. An illness had destroyed that too. First polio, then the ovarian infection caused by a rare and uncontrollable virus that had closed both of her Fallopian tubes, making her definitely infertile, the physician had confirmed. Wherever she looked: nothing but dead ends in her life. At any rate, consistently. One crippling illness led to another. That's how her father had seen it.

Roswitha's hands are still aching. She still finds it hard to grab anything. In the night she had stolen away from his side into the kitchen, turned on the light and observed her hands, panic-stricken. She couldn't move her fingers properly any more. Their delicate joints were red and swollen. Roswitha immersed both hands in cool water. She was only able to hold the pitcher with difficulty. Afterwards she found a medicated ointment in the cabinet, rubbed it on the joints and wrapped them in soft flannel. Then she didn't go back to Max. She had lain down in her old bed in the workshop. She had clasped her bandaged hands over her breast. Later she noticed pain in her lower abdomen, as if her abdominal wall were criss-crossed with welts.

The former agility of her fingers is not yet restored. And her knuckles are still swollen. Nevertheless, she goes to the effort of cutting the bread for him. She does feel that she should change something, should refuse to comply with him, but on the one hand she is too dejected to do anything, on the other hand she calms herself with the thought that everything was just a misunderstanding.

At the table, she is across from Max as usual and sees the part in his hair. He always sits hunched over when he eats, as if he had to push his face into the trough like an animal. She has only seen him proud and upright between the rails on the ties. As Max picks up the coffee mug with both hands and raises it to drink, she takes a good look at his hands for the first time. His short, wide fingers have blond hair on them. His fingernails are short and torn, the wide bed of the nail almost overgrown by the cuticle. Those are hands that can grab hold, that grabbed hold every night, that had explored and rumpled up her body; they are unscathed. Roswitha's hands are still protected by the soft bandages. She sees them lying before her, her beautiful hands, inelegantly wrapped in gooey gauze, perhaps disfigured for ever. Again she feels like crying. At first she tries to suppress a sob, but then it breaks out of her and she bursts into tears. That is aimed at Max. As he leaves, he thumps her on the side: Now, now! he says and is out of the apartment. Roswitha runs into the bedroom, lies down in bed again and sleeps another hour. When she finally gets up late in the morning, the events of the night, like those of breakfast, have receded into the distance. So far away as if they had taken place in another life or in a film that she had once seen. It no longer seems to have happened to her. She removes the bandage from her hands; her fingers are as white and slender as ever, they have suffered no permanent damage. And their agility has almost entirely returned.

 In the evening, Roswitha waits in vain again for Max. She has set the table, but he doesn't come. So she eats alone. Today is the first meeting with the theater troupe. Lotte will pick her up. Roswitha has to get ready. Soon she has forgotten Max. She collects her sketches, changes her clothes, and is already at the meeting in thought, trying to imagine how it will be.

 The school inspector seems to have been waiting for her. He hurries toward her with open arms: How good of you to come! Lotte has told me so much about you. Lotte smiles. And he greets her too. The parish hall is a high, whitewashed room with ornamental plasterwork on the ceiling, in which the few little tables seem lost. Several strong young country lads have already gathered there. They are his extras, the inspector explains, gesturing with his hand toward the group that is sitting in rows on the benches along the wall. The librarian of the parish lending library, Miss Greta, has obviously also been chosen to play a role in the play. She is sitting somewhat to the side at one of the smaller tables, where Lotte with Roswitha and the inspector now take their places.

Hingerl holds the chair for Roswitha. Who does she think she is now, sitting beside the schoolteacher who was already a teacher, a person to be respected, when she was in public school? At this small table the hierarchical order has disappeared. Roswitha as an equal beside the director off duty, the member of the Church Council and District Council, the author. The inspector has good posture and makes a youthful impression. His hair is white as snow, but still thick, it is down to his neck, flowing over his coat collar. One can see immediately that he is artistic. Roswitha likes him. He has rosy cheeks and is clean shaven. Well-groomed is what occurs to Roswitha, that's what he is. He probably also smells a little of fresh aftershave. His Roman nose, wide chin and dark bushy eyebrows over his bright eyes make a great impression on Roswitha because they are so masculine. Hingerl laughs and she sees his white, even teeth. They are certainly his third set, but how attractive! Roswitha secretly enthuses. She also recognizes the good cut of his green hunting suit. A girl from the Catholic Parish Youth comes with a tray offering them glasses of apple juice and wine. The inspector stands up and summarizes the reason for their coming together. For the 1000-year celebration of the marketplace he has written an historical tragedy that plays in the Middle Ages and deals with a recorded memorable event. In a few days, he will distribute the scripts to the individual actors. He goes on to talk about the rehearsal times and the performance date. Then Roswitha hears her name. Hingerl mentions her because she is prepared to sew the costumes for his drama, and he thanks her very much for that in advance. Later he speaks directly to Roswitha and invites her to take the measurements of the principal actors and the extras right away. After all, most of them are present today. He explains that he himself will play the title role; Lotte Spannring and Greta Schönleithner are the main female actors. It is about the tension of an eternal triangle in medieval days. He will figure as the knight crusader between two women, namely his spouse, played by Miss

Greta, who is libeled by a despicable letter written by an envious person, and a beautiful Gypsy, played by Mrs. Lotte, who endeavors to seduce him. Everyone listens raptly. The extras are primarily pages and lady's maids, whose significance for the decoration and success of the undertaking cannot be overestimated, above all because they will be wearing historically accurate garments. I myself, he adds, have already sketched the costumes based on what I know and how I imagine them to be. So in closing he just has to ask the costume designer, he bows playfully to Roswitha, if she feels she can work according to his designs? Roswitha is blushing of course and, pulled into the limelight so unexpectedly, is unable to answer. She can only nod. Lotte comes to her rescue: Naturally Roswitha will do that, she knows how. I'll vouch for that. Bravo, bravo, laughs the inspector. Roswitha is clinging to her measuring tape. Into this relaxed, happy atmosphere comes another visitor through the door. As a member of the Church Council and for today as the representative of the Reverend Father, he is invited to their table by the inspector. It's Bruno, who takes a place beside the librarian. Roswitha is very surprised; that embarrasses her. Bruno gives her a fleeting nod. He doesn't seem particularly pleased to find his sister-in-law here either. Still, he is obviously feeling fine again.

Hingerl now asks Roswitha to go to work. She takes out her measuring tape, her notebook and pencil, things that she always carried with her, and starts to take the measurements of the extras. They are four boys and two girls from the Catholic Parish Youth between the ages of sixteen and eighteen, who smile with embarrassment as they wait for her. Roswitha doesn't know anyone. As she uses her measuring tape her confusion disappears. She is on familiar ground again. She is good at her profession, and that lends her confidence.

One after the other gets up from the bench as soon as it is his or her turn, and stands in front of the tailor who goes to work with her pencil behind her ear, the measuring tape in her hands. She measures the bust, neck size and hips, waist, for the boys also the pant length, the width of their back, sleeve length and so on.

Taking measurements involves getting close to people. One

penetrates their intimate sphere, so to speak. When you are measuring them, nothing escapes you. Almost nothing. But Roswitha has long since given up wanting to know something about the other people. The different personal odors are of as little interest to her as the different length and width measurements. She no longer lets herself be irritated by the closeness of her customers. So the work goes quickly. The girls giggle with embarrassment or stare straight ahead over Roswitha when she is taking their bust measurement and lining up the tape measure across their breasts. She notes the measurement discreetly. She has even long since stopped herself from whispering the numbers to help her remember them. She puts a name in front of every row of numbers.

After the extras come the principal actors. She already has the measurements for Lotte and the librarian because both are her customers. So only the inspector remains, who plants himself quickly in front of her when it is his turn. Roswitha puts her tape measure around him; she has to stand on her toes to reach his neck and shoulders, and almost kneel down in front of him to measure the inner pant length. She almost has to embrace him to measure the circumference of his chest, waist and hips. The man actually does smell a little of men's cologne. Perhaps of Speick. Although Roswitha avoids looking the inspector in the face, she senses that he is watching her. She also notices movement in his body, which is in her hands for a short time, as soon as he turns his head or looks down or up. She notices each of his head movements either in his shoulder blades, his hips or even his legs. She notices that he is bending forward and looking at her back as she stoops down. She reminds him: Please stay standing up straight; otherwise I will get false measurements. Pardon, pardon! he says in a loud and cheerful voice.

She has finished measuring his body, wants to pack up her things, roll up her measuring tape, when the school inspector reaches for her hands and asks her if he can look at them. Her hands now lie on his palms, he looks at the backs of her hands, then turns her hands over with the greatest of care so that he has the inner sides before him, and shakes his head admiringly. He says aloud: Indeed, I have never in my life seen such perfectly formed hands. Flawless! Take good care of them, such hands, such fingers are a treasure, do you know that? Roswitha, who feels like someone to whom justice has suddenly been done, kneads the back of her hands in her excitement. The teacher laughs: Don't hide them, please! Grant us the sight of them! He turns to the table: Maybe I can work these hands into my play. How would it be if a seductive Gypsy were to give me, the knight Hartmut, a sign by waving a white kerchief from a window? Lotte, you will excuse me if I have this scene done by your double? He laughs again. Greta and Lotte laugh with him, uncertain whether they should take Hingerl's suggestion seriously. Bruno grins. Roswitha is beaming, and feels almost faint with happiness.

When she is then standing alone in the cool night, she no longer knows how she got out of the parish hall or whether she said good-bye to everyone. She has gaps in her memory as if she's had a concussion; because the inspector – she clasps this memory like a pillow to her breast – said "Allow me" and kissed her hand in parting.

Roswitha walks carefully through the parish garden. A narrow path crosses it since the construction work began. Lotte has stayed behind with the inspector. She has various things to discuss with him about her role. And Bruno has probably accompanied Miss Greta home.

Roswitha holds her hands into the dim light of the rising moon, unspeakably happy at the prospect of having them appear in the play. She is reeling, as if a horn of plenty were pouring out its contents over her head. This feeling that she is being rewarded for her goodness by riches raining down on her makes her contemptuous of past things; she dismisses her thought of death that had been a comfort to her for years. This moment has put everything right, has made good all her expectations. Her former weariness with life now seems sinful to her. Today the value of her existence has been confirmed. Whatever lies ahead of her, whatever may yet come can no longer frighten her. She thinks of Max with the forgiving nature of the happy. At the same time, she recognizes that she took a false step when she let herself in with him. She cannot stay together with Max. Her life has taken a different path, away from unskilled construction workers and people who walk the tracks on their day off; she is striving toward something higher.

From a distance she sees that there is light in her apartment. All the rooms are brightly lit. The light from the windows falls on the scaffolding, whose shadows resemble bars and give the house the appearance of being dilapidated.

The light in her windows makes Roswitha uneasy. Previously she was always touched in a friendly fashion by lamplight in the dark of night.

So Max is still awake. Or did he forget to turn out the lights? That's what she hopes, until she hears the noise. Men's yelling, singing and laughter mix with the coarse droning of an accordion. She has to stand still and catch her breath on the stairs. Her knees are trembling. She doesn't want to surrender the good and beautiful things that have come her way today. That is her treasure that must give her the strength to resist the lowness of the unskilled construction worker and his buddies.

She will have to go up and in. Put an end to the goings-on. Once and for all. How embarrassing and disgraceful if the inspector, this sensitive author and gentleman, were to find out something about her acquaintances.

The door to the apartment is unlocked. From the hall, which is in a fog of cigarette smoke, she looks through the open door to the sewing room. I am in a strange apartment, it flashes through her mind for a moment. Or am I dreaming? Is the dream of happiness now followed by the nightmare? She can't say what disturbs her most when she walks in: the deafening din, the dirt on the linoleum, the thick clouds of smoke, the rumpled rug, or the chair tipped over by the door. From the doorway, there are no people to be seen.

She only stands there briefly in a daze, then she limps, crippled, into the midst of the devastation and curses her affliction. They haven't heard her come. Roswitha stands in her workshop, which for decades was very precious to her, the most important thing. Its inventory had grown around her according to her needs, customs and preferences. She could find her way around blind in the room.

The bed and beside it the dresser, the table she used for cutting, beside it the sewing machine, the folding screen for the customers changing their clothes, the tailor's dummy next to the window, on which she had put the librarian's dirndl dress, chests of sewing things, measuring tapes and silk threads, scissors in various sizes and of various sharpness, chalks, sewing needles, pins and safety-pins, on the dresser in little drawers buttons and zippers, selvage tapes, bias binding and elastic bands. There was a place for everything. The order in her workspace was always of utmost importance to her. She was proud of the ingenious system she had devised. Security, permanence and safety were closely linked with this functional, clear arrangement. Nothing remains of it now. The men still haven't noticed Roswitha. Three fellows have their backs to her. She has a side view of a fourth, the one with the accordion. He has a beard, the sweat is running down his face and out of his arm pits, and he has rolled up the sleeves of his blue plaid shirt so that she can see his hairy arms with blue tattoos. With one hand he presses on the round buttons of his instrument, with the other he squeezes the bellows. She hears a march. The tailor's dummy is now standing in the middle of the room next to the dresser. The three men have set themselves up across from it. They are holding knives in their hands; other knives are lying on the table, from which her sewing utensils have disappeared. Instead, there are beer bottles and ashtrays on it.

The men have chosen the tailor's dummy with the librarian's dirndl dress on it as their target. Several knives are already sticking into the red bodice. Several are lying scattered on the floor. Max has just thrown his knife and hit the left breast. All four men howl, stamp their feet and leap up, hug each other, thump Max on the shoulder and reach for the bottles of beer. With the bottles in their hands, they turn around and finally discover Roswitha.

As a young girl, Roswitha went regularly to the movies. She preferred comedies and love stories with happy endings, films with moments of surprise and surprise entries. Roswitha liked the actors' reaction in an unexpected meeting, their having to look twice in disbelief. She as a member of the audience knew what was going on and snorted with amusement at the person who was duped. So when people who were thought to be dead or away on a trip unexpectedly turned up, the astonishment of the person who was taken by surprise had to be in proportion to the unexpectedness of the appearance. Such scenes made Roswitha laugh and cheered her up.

Today she herself has become part of such a scene, knowing what is going on and acting in it at the same time. In spite of her being so disturbed, she is also seized by a sort of stage-fright; she thinks the suddenness of her appearance will work to her advantage.

So the men have noticed her, but they only glance briefly at her. They don't stare in confusion like in the movies; don't stutter in embarrassment as if caught in the act, they simply don't pay attention to her. Even Max has only a fleeting nod for her. Not one of them is bothered by her being there. The intruders bend to pick up their knives; one of them pulls his out of the dummy. The upper part of the dirndl dress is already punctured by several hits. However, the two tips of the breasts, where the men have put star-shaped marks with white chalk, remain untouched. These points are obviously the main targets of their missiles.

Now, as when she entered, Roswitha has the men's backs in front of her. Max is the largest of them. One is slim and nervous; the others are burly and slow. So Roswitha stares at the three backs, one of which is known to her and the two others belong to strangers; under their thin shirts the shoulder blades stand out moist. The accordion player keeps on playing.

They start to throw again. Max hits the fastener in the middle, but the knife doesn't stick in, it crashes to the floor.

Then Roswitha screams: Stop!

Finally the men turn around. She looks into their faces, some astonished, some amused. The accordion player stops playing.

The ground is rocking under Roswitha's feet, but she still stumbles a few steps toward Max: Get out!

The men look at Max undecidedly. He makes a dismissive motion with his hand. The slight one with the dark hair wants to calm Roswitha down: But who's getting so grumpy!

You'll clear off this instant, immediately, on the spot, you understand? she screams, her voice breaking. Finally she has the right rage.

The accordion player quickly packs his instrument in its case. Max stamps toward her: Now, what, what then, what d'ya want? What then? Now, what? What. What?

Roswitha bends down, grabs one of the delicately slim knives and goes for Max with it. He backs up slowly step by step in front of the stuck out blade, his grin freezes on his face. Roswitha drives him as far as the exit door. So, she says, so, so, so. And takes her hobbling steps. The others have cleared out in the meantime. When Max is standing with his back to the wall, Roswitha breathes a sign of relief, there is an unspeakably pleasant tingling in her stomach from sheer triumph, and she doesn't know what to do next. Then he grabs her by the wrist, snatches the knife from her and shoves her to the floor. Then he starts to wreak havoc. He smashes bottles and glasses on the partition, throws chairs against the wall. Roswitha flees into the corridor and locks herself in the lavatory. She considers calling for help. She already has the window open to scream for help into the night.

But the darkness surrounding her, the guards marching behind barbed wire out of earshot, and lastly the thought that Max would become aware of her again and might threaten her, all make her keep silent. In the meantime, it has become quiet again in the apartment. So she sneaks out of the lavatory, which now seems to her like a trap. Freezing and listening, she waits a while in the dark corridor. Everything is quiet. She thinks again of the school inspector who kissed her hand. The thought makes her so happy and so sad that she might almost have started to cry if she weren't afraid of making a noise. For a while she waits, trembling; when nothing more is moving, she sneaks to the door and opens it quietly.

He is no longer in the workshop, where there is still a light on. She crosses the room on the tips of her toes, trying to avoid the broken glass, bottles, the turned over chairs. The tailor's dummy with the torn dirndl dress is lying on the floor, blocking the way. With an effort, Roswitha climbs over it. There is still light on in the hall as well.

Max is sitting in the kitchen. He is holding his head in both his hands and mumbling to himself. Roswitha doesn't understand a word. His head sinks slowly onto the table top. He has probably fallen asleep. She still doesn't dare to enter the kitchen. She has no choice but to do without getting washed. She sneaks tiredly away. Although she is afraid of Max, she has to lie in the double bed. Her workshop is so terribly ravaged; Max's fit of rage hasn't even spared her bed; the cushions and quilt are bunched up on the floor in the midst of the broken glasses. Today she no longer has the strength to clean up and remove what has been vandalized. Would she ever have the strength again? She lies on the double bed and thinks she will never want to get up again; the highpoint was simultaneously the end of her life, she thinks and feels as if she is going to be sick. If she were to die now: the school inspector would give the funeral oration, she was sure of that now, he would remember how her hands were without equal in beauty and shapeliness. In this manner she would remain in the memories of the village inhabitants for a long time. These thoughts are a comfort to her, and she falls asleep.

She has slept very deeply. When she wakes up, there is already bright morning light. The place by her side is empty. The rumpled pillows show that Max must have lain beside her. Roswitha lies still and tries to remember yesterday. The happy event is instantly there again, and she strokes her hands; then gradually the horror and helplessness of the other incidents appear. There is nothing to be heard in the apartment, only a knocking and hammering coming from outside. Roswitha leaps out of bed. Obviously they are already at work. Max has left the house without waking her, probably also without anything in his stomach. That was considerate of him. Maybe he is ashamed of his behavior and has snuck out of the house full of regret. Who knows, maybe he has such a bad conscience that he'll keep out of my sight. That would be no great loss, Roswitha says to herself. She is now no longer thinking of bidding him an unconditional farewell. But she'll at least threaten him with it, she'll hold up to him the possibility of getting kicked out, like putting a birch rod in the window.

Later, when she is kneeling on the floor and picking up the

pieces of broken glass, she thinks of her father, who impressed on her from early childhood that she would never get a man. Each time he said so it was just a dry observation. For that reason, he used to announce, he had given her mother instructions not to bring her up as a girl. She would have to fend for herself at some point. Therefore, she should learn an occupation, preferably one she could do sitting down. So he came up with the occupation of a dressmaker. Even her mother had never doubted that her younger daughter would end up an old maid. They just had to get used to it. To that purpose, her father had also never seen anything feminine in her, neither fish nor fowl, as he said. He had been very sober with her, treating her like an item of practical use. Roswitha was in agreement with that. She loved her father. She had liked being in his hands. When she got polio at the age of three and it was certain she would remain a cripple, he had told her mother to take down the picture of the Mother of God with the baby Jesus in her arms and to hang up instead the heart of Mary pierced with seven swords. That, Roswitha says to herself today, is proof to me that my father loved me.

Roswitha, still kneeling on the floor, collecting things, wiping and polishing up, is smiling with satisfaction. She has got a man quite without any effort on her part. He dropped in unexpectedly. Besides, she had already become something without a man; she got the man as a bonus, as a luxury object. As something superfluous? She can keep him or throw him out, just as she wishes. Is that what her father wanted for her? Roswitha is sure that he would be pleased to see her have so much power. But I can't put that at risk without giving it a thought, she considers. Of course she is still kneeling on the floor, stooping and bending over the mess, struggling with the confusion, fighting the dirt in a humble manner which that very man has forced on her. While picking up the pieces of broken glass, she inadvertently cuts her finger. The blood drips onto the light-colored cloth she is using for cleaning. It reminds Roswitha of a fairy-tale: as white as snow, as red as blood. She puts the injured index finger in her mouth, settles herself down on the soiled carpet, leans back against the table leg, puts her head back, shuts her eyes, sucks and bites at the wound, while she dances around with her other hand before her now opened eyes. Again she feels the familiar state of euphoria that drives her into a frenzy and passion. When it is over, she stands up awkwardly and looks for a Band-Aid because the wound is bleeding more than before. And now it also hurts. Roswitha nods, because that's how it should be. Afterwards everything hurts. That is the price.

Now she hurries to get finished with the major part of the work. She fetches a broom and sweeps everything into a pile without further ado. Max will have to reimburse her for the damage. She casts a glance out her workshop window. Max just happens to be busy with a shovel and wheelbarrow directly underneath her window. Through the droning of the excavator, she thinks she hears his labored breathing, although she can only see his bent back. She is touched again by his busy working, above all his bent back makes her soft-hearted.

When Max comes for lunch he says he is feeling sick today, he isn't hungry. Roswitha brings him the washbasin, soap and towel. Afterwards she shows him her workshop, which she has only straightened up in a makeshift fashion, tells him how many glasses were smashed, shows him the pile of pieces of broken glass and the punctured dirndl dress. Max acts remorseful. He doesn't remember anything any more. He was probably too drunk. The spirits that Kurti Schweinschwaller brought always made him so violent. It would never happen again. He would of course compensate her for the damages. Roswitha was so relieved she could have shouted; but she growled, apparently only partially appeased, well, alright, but if it happens again, then ... He nods, he knows.

Then Max's appetite does return and he takes large helpings of the potato pancakes. Afterwards he brings out a bill from the bedroom that should, he thinks, be enough to compensate for the damages, including the dirndl dress. The amount, Roswitha estimates it in an instant, is not enough. She takes the bill and sighs, well, alright. She will have to sew a new bodice for the dirndl dress. Her time is not included in the amount. But she doesn't want to be so petty. After all, Max has shown remorse and is trying to make amends.

In the afternoon, Roswitha continues trying to make her

workshop usable again. That depresses her and she has second thoughts about whether it was right to let herself be placated by a mere 1000 schillings. The damage done has cost her at least a complete day at her work. For the first time, she will not be able to deliver the articles of clothing on time. As a tailor, she has always placed a great deal of importance on punctuality, on being absolutely reliable. Her customers value these qualities, as she knows. The matter with the dirndl dress is particularly unpleasant for her; she was supposed to have it ready for tomorrow, Friday. And now – she sees no other way about it – she will have to prepare Greta for a delay. What if the disappointed customer told the school inspector that she was in arrears with her work, and if he, concerned about the success of his drama, to which the costumes should contribute in no insignificant way, were to take the honorable commission away from her again? Or even if he were to find out that she was living together with a man in so-called "sin!" The inspector is a regular churchgoer and zealously receives communion. He is without question a man of honor in the village. Roswitha is now almost sorry that she didn't get things straight with Max; it would still have been possible to get rid of Max without too much fuss. Certainly the sympathy of those who knew would have been entirely with her. Roswitha thinks that over as she gathers up the scattered sewing needles, the pins and safety-pins, the tangled threads and the crumbled tailor's chalk and puts them back in the right boxes. She also finds two knives, which she brings to the chest in the bedroom. Then the doorbell rings.

It's Martha. Roswitha is embarrassed, because she knows her room still shows traces of the wild scene there the night before. Her sister says right away that she doesn't want to stay long. What a sight it is outside! Soon there won't be a stone left standing, she says and goes into the kitchen. She asks for a glass of water. Roswitha wants to know how her sister is feeling.

How should I be feeling? she snaps back.

What does the doctor say? Roswitha asks.

He says one thing, then another thing.

Roswitha is annoyed. What does her sister want here anyway? She sighs, thinking of the interrupted work.

I might be going into hospital, or I might not, I might let myself be operated, I might be dead the day after tomorrow, says Martha and laughs a little.

She's fooling me. She's been fooling me all my life. You never know with her.

That's all nonsense! Roswitha snaps at her.

I might let them cut me away, bit by bit, until there is nothing left.

Just listen to you! Roswitha has had enough.

Then you aren't a woman any more, when everything is gone, broods Martha.

Such nonsense, Roswitha bursts out, as if the breast were everything about you.

It's easy for you to talk, says Martha and stands up. So where is he then, your man? It's because of him that I came. I do want to meet your future husband. What time does he get home?

Roswitha says that Max always works overtime. But her sister can see him from the window; he is working directly under the hall window. Actually Max is sitting under the walnut tree taking a break.

From a distance quite presentable, Martha thinks, so how is he then?

Things are working out alright, Roswitha says evasively.

Aha, says Martha and laughs a little. Who would have thought that you would still get a man. It's too funny.

Yes, says Roswitha, that it is.

I'm going now, says Martha.

Come sometime with Bruno, says Roswitha.

He has no time. He's always away, says Martha.

Well then, good-bye, says Roswitha.

Farewell, says Martha.

Roswitha breathes a sigh of relief when her sister is out of the apartment. It was always difficult to get along with her, Roswitha remembers, I have never understood her. She never let me get close to her. Even when our parents were suddenly dead and I wanted to see mother and father in her, she kept aloof from me. She did guide me, and steer me, but from a distance, more bureaucratically. I froze beside her. But without her I probably wouldn't have survived the first few years. She probably kept me alive. That obliges me to be grateful. Or to ask. I don't ask her the right questions, Roswitha realizes, how should I find out more from her? Then she stops worrying about her sister, because she has enough problems of her own.

Today Max comes straight home from work. No pub today. He seems to be serious with his good intentions. Roswitha notices how she relaxes, how she gradually even forgets the devastation in her workshop. Order is in any case almost completely restored. A *faux pas*, well, when living together with a man you probably had to take a few of those in your stride. They eat the evening meal together. Then Roswitha has to go to her sewing machine to catch up on the work she has promised for tomorrow. She is content in her cone of light, where she is doing embroidery. She is looking forward to next Wednesday, when the second meeting is supposed to take place. By then she will be able to make suggestions about materials. Everything seems to be running smoothly at last with Max. When he behaves decently, she no longer needs to be ashamed of him. He is a handsome man. Now she will press for marriage in the near future, because the village won't tolerate the present arrangement for long. She, as a single woman, has to pay particular attention to her reputation. And now of all times, since her assistance with the play will soon put her in the public eye.

Although her bed in the workshop is clean and smooth again, she still goes to lie with Max. He has turned himself on his back and is already snoring. That prevents her from falling asleep for a long time. Later he wakes up and feels his way through the room to the lavatory. When he comes back, he reaches for her; she has just fallen asleep and is too sleepy to resist him, which in any case has not proven to be effective. He grabs her lower abdomen, which she indifferently lets him have. He gets tangled up in her nightgown and finally in her underpants. Since the items of clothing seem to have a will of their own, more so than usual, he starts to swear quietly. Roswitha is now entirely awake, because he is hurting her. She whimpers quietly, then finally screams and tries to get away from him. But to no avail, he has already pinned her to the sheet. It occurs to her that he has never kissed her. His breath is wheezing in her ear. Strangely, in addition to the pain, over the stinging and burning, she feels the first stirring of desire, against which she struggles. She wants to stick to her suffering, which seems appropriate to her situation. Also, she is confused by the simultaneity of pain and desire. So she lies quite still and denies herself. Unexpectedly, she thinks of the inspector and his mustache. Then her feelings become entirely muddled. She imagines that the school inspector would kiss her on the mouth, as a result, a wave of ecstasy surges up from her womb, which she tries in vain to suppress, but which helps Max quickly to a blazing finish.

For a long time, Roswitha remains lying in the position she was in when he pulled out of her, and thinks about herself. She no longer knows at all anymore what she wants, what she should want. Only after she puts her hands on her forehead and cheeks does she feel calmer again. She thinks ardently of the inspector and considers whether she should put nail polish on her fingernails to make her hands have an even more irresistible effect on him.

Max has just left the house to go to work, and Roswitha is clearing off the breakfast table when she is startled by the siren with its hair-raising howling. She dashes excitedly to the window, thinking there is a fire. If it were just an exercise by the fire department, she would be disappointed, because she has gotten such a fright from the sustained, continuous wailing high and low that only a catastrophe could be in keeping with it. Her nerves are ready for a rather large disaster. First she runs to the window in the hall and opens the casements. Meanwhile, the siren has stopped, but far or near there is neither a red glow nor smoke to be seen. Also, none of the workers is in front of the house. So she flits to her workshop window. Here there seems to be something going on. The workmen are standing there too, with their backs to her, as if they were rooted to the spot. Their heads are tipped back and they are staring upwards. An airplane? No. Roswitha sees that the guards in front of the prison wing, instead of patrolling as usual, are standing still with their rifle barrels presented upwards. She catches sight of Max, who is also gaping upwards and holding his hand over his eyes as a shield, she wants to call him and ask what is going on, but then she discovers that there are human figures moving on the roof of the church. Two men in prisoner's clothing are obviously crawling on the large hipped roof, clinging to the snow guard. A skylight is standing open. They must have climbed out of it. Meanwhile, several police cars have come racing up with their sirens blaring and take up position in the parish garden. The officers leap out and drive the workmen back. They are forbidden to continue working. Soon an ambulance arrives as well, and a barred green paddy wagon, a so-called "green Henry." More police spring out of the vehicles and take up position in the garden with their weapons cocked. Others start to close the area with a mesh fence. Roswitha is astonished at how quickly and quietly everything happens, as if it were a conspiracy.

Only a few minutes have elapsed since Roswitha was startled by the siren, and already people are thronging the parish garden. The barrier is not yet entirely impassable, so they slip through and gather in small groups. They shout excitedly, wave their arms, and also watch and observe what is going on up over their heads at a dizzying height, 50 meters[2] above firm ground. The prisoners' clothing is almost the same color as the gray slate roof, and it is not easy to discern exactly what is happening up there. The people call loudly for telescopes, which the police of course have and which they have set up on tripods at appropriate places, but they are not accessible to the unauthorized audience.

Max comes in. He too asks for binoculars. Roswitha knows she still has her father's binoculars and looks for them. Meanwhile he is standing at the window and staring up to the two figures that have let themselves down above the snow guard. The masons, who are now not allowed to continue working, have climbed up the scaffolding and made themselves comfortable right under Roswitha's window. They greet Max like someone who enjoys the privilege of a box seat in the theater. Roswitha lugs over an old-fashioned pair of field glasses that Max takes out of her hands right away. The men under the window also stretch out their arms for the field glasses. Roswitha feels the little opera glasses in her apron

---
[2] 165 feet

pocket, which she found beside the field glasses, and which her mother had once been given by a kind lady for whom she cleaned. Roswitha just wants to use them in secret, so that they too don't disappear into strange hands. In the meantime, Roswitha tries to recognize details with her naked eye. The two men are sitting apparently motionless on the roof and letting their legs hang over the snow guard. Roswitha feels dizzy when she looks at them and imagines how far down they could plunge. Maybe the men are suicidal. Max seems to be considering the same thing, because he says, still with the field glasses before his eyes, that they had better jump soon if they intend to, because otherwise the fire department will come with the life net. One of the construction workers on the scaffolding, who hears Max, interjects that when someone jumps from such a height the life net wouldn't help worth a damn; he'd break his neck.

Meanwhile, someone sticks his head out the skylight; it's an official head with a peaked cap that seems to be talking insistently to the escaped prisoners. Max reports that the men are shaking their heads. Then he slaps his thighs and laughs and claims that he knows one of them, he's a crook, a bank robber, he had thrown knives with him once in Hinterstoder, or was it in Losenstein, and Max had won against him. Soon after that the guy had been arrested. That was Egon Blahowetz, he was entirely certain. He was an idiot, only an idiot would seat himself on the roof, there was no way out of there. Max smiles importantly.

Finally Roswitha also gets to look through the glass. She is shocked to have the two figures suddenly apparently within reach, in her room, so to speak. She has the two so close in front of her that she can see their pores, at the mercy of her keyhole view. She is ashamed, but still stares at their faces, a young one and an old one. Max has identified the one as a serious offender. But the other one, a pale boy, twenty years old at most, who is sliding around behind the snow guard, what could have landed him in prison?

Max gets himself set up at the window, because there can be no more thought of working until further notice. Part of the parish garden is cordoned off by police and gendarmerie. Guards and police officers armed with rifles and pistols also position themselves in the remaining part of the garden; they take up position between pieces of construction equipment and behind piles of cement and gravel. In the meantime, a vehicle of the Austrian Broadcasting Company has also arrived. Journalists are questioning individual executive officers. Max asks for a radio; Roswitha has to admit that she doesn't own one, then Max curses and says that she really does still live in the Middle Ages. At this key word Roswitha jumps almost joyfully.

A doctor and nurses in white smocks stand around the ambulance. More and more curious people crowd along the barrier into the garden. Max gets thirsty, he calls for beer. Roswitha shrugs her shoulders; she doesn't have any on hand. Max curses again. He sits at the window and smacks himself angrily on the thighs. Suddenly he jumps up, waves his arms and calls out: Fred, Kurt! Come here! Roswitha, who has just gone back into the kitchen, hears the doorbell. When she opens the door, the two men she still has bad memories about are standing outside. They drag in a case of beer. Max is on the spot immediately, pushes Roswitha aside and ushers the two into the living room with a great show of courtesy. Roswitha has never seen Max so excited.

She reasons: Two convicts – how and why one still doesn't know – have climbed onto the church roof and have thus once again turned her day upside down, so that she can't say what will happen. What is still possible and what not? How much freedom of movement does she still have after they have taken the liberty up there of climbing out on the roof? Her workshop, in any case, is occupied again. What does she have to do with the two criminals on the roof? How is it possible that the appearance of these people completely unknown to her can halt the normal and well-ordered course of her day? Roswitha sits at the table to think it over. The event that is ruining her schedule is really no concern of hers. The fact that it nevertheless affects her is due solely to the location of her apartment. If she lived even a hundred yards away in a little one-storey house with no view of the crime scene, she would be able to carry out her work undisturbed, no one would occupy her window or her workshop.

It's not as if the two men who are climbing about at a dizzying height right in front of her leave her completely cold. Even if she still lived alone, she would certainly have sat at the window and watched what was happening, and perhaps have done some light sewing at the same time. It would have been quite comfortable. But now that the men have forced their way into her apartment again, her observation seat by the window is taken and her workshop occupied. She will have to regard the day as a lost workday. She will get shamefully behind with her work and not have it ready on time. Her clientele might conceivably transfer to the competition, because that is lurking in the form of a ladies' and gentlemen's tailor who is shrewd and quick. As she imagines these dark prospects and sees that nothing can be changed at the moment and she will have to make the best of it, she decides at least to watch the drama, which does promise to get exciting. After all, she wouldn't have the opportunity every day to watch two people, even if they were criminals, on the roof of the church in a life-threatening situation. She wants to find out the how and why. Maybe Max knows more. So she leaves the kitchen and goes to the men.

They have made themselves comfortable in a semi-circle at the window so that all three of them have a good view of the happenings on the church roof.

Max is just now discussing the situation with one of his work-mates who is sitting on the scaffolding. From him he finds out that people are saying the two escapees had broken through a relatively thin wall that separates the prison wing from the church. Because of the construction work taking place all around, no one had heard their banging and hammering. They had been in the process of escaping into the open through the sacristy when the sexton discovered them and they had run away from the man, who was raising the hue and cry, into the inner part of the church. However, the intrepid pursuer had driven them higher and higher up until they finally reached the attic, from where they had crawled through a skylight onto the roof. Now, from up there, they were sending out their extortionate demands: Apparently they wanted safe-conduct, a getaway vehicle, civilian clothing and a million schillings. Otherwise they would jump. Someone else said that he had heard that the two had made the request that they be allowed to report on the radio about the unreasonable conditions, as they put it, in the prison, and to inform the public about the inhumane treatment to which they were subjected, and the harassment. They had prepared a 100-page paper that they wished to broadcast on the radio.

Max and his friends are incensed about the criminals' boldness; then everyone could demand that. But they also laugh about the roof climbers and shake their heads, raise their bottles to each other and drink one bottle of beer after another.

Roswitha, who wants to be noticed by the men, comments that the two at least possess courage to stay out there at such a dizzying height in a cramped position. They had to hold on the whole time to the snow guard, which was already very rusty, as could be seen through the binoculars.

Max says to the two others that it is typical of a woman to like something like that. And with that, Roswitha feels that he has noticed her.

The doorbell rings. It's Lotte, who asks the surprised Roswitha if she can "watch" at her place. Hermann was called in to work, since they now need everyone, so that the two escapees can be delivered back into custody safe and sound.

Quite embarrassed, Roswitha leads her friend into the room to the three men. But contrary to her fears, they receive Lotte enthusiastically. The semi-circle is expanded. Roswitha brings over a chair for the newcomer and a glass, because Max, who is putting on airs as the head of the household and the host, immediately offers ma'am a beer. Lotte thinks that a glass of beer can't hurt, after all people are sweating a lot today. She is also allowed to look through the field glass; then a head appears in the skylight again, and she screams: There he is, that's Hermann! He's already negotiating with the convicts. They don't want any bloodshed, she explains to Max, and cheers: The parish priest beside my Hermann. Even the Reverend Father has to suffer! They all see two heads in the narrow skylight, one with a peaked cap and one with a bare head. The two heads move, and from a distance it looks as if they are jovially bumping into each other like in a Punch and Judy show. Through the opera glass, which Roswitha now dares to take out because the others are starring spellbound at the church roof, the matter certainly looks different; the pastor's serious facial expression and Hermann's grim wrath destroy any such happy thought. Roswitha thinks she notices that the men move respectfully a little away from her friend, who is the wife of a prison guard, and it enrages Roswitha that now, in addition to the escapees, Lotte too has become the center of attention. For her there is now no more room at the window. So she positions herself two steps behind Max and dares to pull the opera glass out of her apron pocket. The glass is small and dainty. She presses it to her eyes. To make it not so easy for anyone to discover her treasure and demand it from her, she masks it under her hands. Soon she has the focus correctly adjusted and now looks for the escapees. The men and Lotte are also trying intently to keep them in view; they take turns using the field glass. The rebels occasionally move about now, they feel their way on all fours a few steps along the snow guard, or they lie down. Every one of their movements is commented on by the gaping people at the window. Roswitha knows that she should now cook the noon meal, but she finally has the young man in view whose name she now also knows. Pius Kiofsky pushes himself along on his knees behind the rusty low railing. Roswitha follows him with her glass. When he is several yards away from his accomplice, with his back to him, he straightens up, fumbles around in his pants – Roswitha has his hands, white and smooth and young, right in sight, they disappear in the prisoner's gray, bring something pale, maggoty-fat to light and let a high, thread-thin arc rain out of it. Roswitha would only too gladly have also been able to watch the boy's face, but Max bellows, he's pissing, he's pissing down on us, just look at that, and Lotte starts to squeal, and Fred wants to tear away the field glass from Max, but he hands it to Lotte, who has already stretched out her hand for it, so that she has something of it too. Roswitha now lets her opera glass disappear quickly into her apron again. Lotte coos as she gapes through the glass, and is all red in the face. Max thumps her in the side, Roswitha thinks she won't like that, then he slaps his thighs and brays with laughter. But Lotte doesn't notice anything at all and doesn't want to tear herself away from the sight. Then Roswitha runs into the kitchen because she suddenly feels sick, and also because she has to prepare a meal. She hopes that the uninvited guests will finally leave. Inwardly, she also feels a growing rage against Lotte who, as it seems to Roswitha, has allied herself with Max and the others against her. She puts a large pot of potatoes on the stove. When she is making the salad, Lotte comes excitedly into the kitchen and announces that her Hermann has resumed the conversation with the convicts; he has now appeared in the skylight with the famous prison psychiatrist Grantzler. When she sees Roswitha busy with the vegetables, she offers to help. She thinks it's wonderful that everything is happening now at Roswitha's place, that this Max has brought life into her life can only be good for Roswitha. They should really have fun now at this chance gathering, Lotte plans, because you have to seize the opportunity, whatever day it falls on. If only they don't fall down, says Roswitha. We don't want to fall down like them, just celebrate, no matter what day it falls on, and not those who fall down. Lotte doubles up with laughter about her play on words. Is that ever funny, she says with tears in her eyes, such a joke. Then she does a good job of helping Roswitha with the cooking, while continuing to talk, and in no time the two of them have a meal ready. Potatoes with curd cheese dressing and salad. Enough for everyone. Roswitha is finally no longer angry.

They eat at Roswitha's work table that they carry to the window so that they don't miss any of the action up there outside. The event shows them to be a group in which even Roswitha feels included. Fred says, and the others agree with him, that it is better than any football game. In the meantime, it has gotten warm outside. The Indian summer sun burns down. Kurti observes that the men up on the roof will be grilled by the heat. Max looks through the field glasses and reports that they have both taken off their jackets and are sitting on them. They'll get sunburn, sunstroke, sunstroke, screams Lotte suddenly and takes the field glasses from Max. Roswitha, too, would like to train her glass on the men's naked upper bodies, but that would be noticed now, so she just stares. But it is of course impossible to make out details from this distance.

And falling down. That's dangerous. They should give up!

Lotte is beside herself with excitement. The young one looks thin, thinks Roswitha, with the opera glass I'm sure I could count his ribs. Then Max discovers with a shout of surprise that the two are now getting some food and drink.

Indeed, something is being let down from the skylight. Max, who now takes the field glasses for himself, shouts indignantly, thinking of his empty plate: chicken, roast chicken, roast chicken and something to drink, that's the limit! The men jump up. Outside something moves in the crowd of people. The people grumble, voices express outrage. Fists are raised in angry gestures. There is unanimous disapproval that the mutinous convicts are being fed, they are doing as they like with the police, the gendarmerie and the judiciary, endangering the constitutional state, breaking the laws, and yet are being fed roast chicken. All are seized by the excitement, and the voice of the people calls in angry chorus, as if rehearsed: Jump, you cowards! Shoot them down, the criminals! The miserable lot! Shoot them down! Down with them! We need another Hitler here, Roswitha hears an older gentleman in traditional costume say to the people around him. Old and young agree with him: Quite so! Exactly! Nothing like this would have happened then.

The explosive atmosphere among the people literally catapults Miss Greta into Roswitha's apartment. No one paid any attention to her ringing the doorbell, so she took the liberty of coming in. That gave Roswitha a fright and made Lotte and especially the men cheer. Roswitha brings yet another chair from the kitchen. Now the places at the window are taken to the last inch. But the neat and trim single woman is squeezed into place at the table with cheers. Thank God she doesn't ask about her dirndl dress. Greta, who as librarian of the parish lending library has much to do with books in her profession, says that until now she has only read about such exciting and upsetting events in novels. She never dreamed that she would ever actually experience such an adventure. But everyone has to use the opportunity and watch. What else? asks Lotte, and Max offers Greta beer that she doesn't refuse. Everyone is thirsty today.

It is the first time Roswitha has been together with so many people who are of one opinion. Each individual is secure in this unanimity. Who would have the courage in such a situation to intercede on behalf of the escapees, to utter even a small word of pity and thereby be excluded from the warm sense of community? Roswitha is nevertheless secretly happy that "her" young man has been given something to eat, and she would like to watch him chewing the meat off the chicken bones and enjoying the food. She wishes him *bon appetit* and quickly reaches for her opera glass, lifts it to her eyes and already has Pius in view. He has just finished his meal and throws down the chicken bones in a wide arc. Since there is no protest, Roswitha assumes that the garbage landed in the eaves trough. She has a quick look at his face and sees him laugh for the first time. He looks at her in the middle of her lens and laughs at her. The laugh belongs to her. She has a secret with him. The five at the window toast each other, and Roswitha lets her opera glass disappear into her apron again.

Meanwhile Greta is telling them that the two men who broke through a wall in their escape attempt damaged a valuable fresco from the 16th century that had just recently undergone a costly restoration, they had damaged it, if not entirely destroyed it. There is unrest in the "soul of the people" in the garden, Roswitha now understands the term, and they are demanding law and order and punishment. Roswitha smiles to herself because she knows her young man is safe up there, they can't reach him. And the police demand that the escapees surrender unconditionally, and ask the people to preserve the peace, or they will be required to leave the garden.

Then the occupants of Roswitha's apartment again become aware of their privileged position, since they can't be driven from the scene.

Roswitha and Lotte carry the dirty dishes into the kitchen. Then all of a sudden Martha is standing in front of them in the hall. Roswitha looks at her sister in astonishment and thinks, that's all I needed! she was here just yesterday; but Lotte is quick to play the lady of the house and ushers Martha into the sewing room, so that she too can have a view of the goings on.

Martha only sees the men's backs and Miss Greta, who turns around and looks her in the face but doesn't say a word, rather turns around right away again, so that she sees only the four backs pressed together in front of her and no room for herself. Then she turns around quickly, dismisses Lotte, leave me be, and finds Roswitha washing dishes alone in the kitchen. Since when has Greta been sitting around at your place, she shouts at her sister. Roswitha shrugs her shoulders, what do I know, she happens to be my client. Oh well, drawls Martha, a client. What's going on again now? asks Roswitha irritably. Martha just wants the key to the attic. What for? The attic room lies directly across from the nave of the church; she will have the best view of the two crazy ones there, smiles Martha.

But the window is so high up that you have to climb a ladder to see out, Roswitha argues, because she suddenly thinks that this lookout also seems useful for her.

She will find a box or a crate among the junk that can be used for that.

As you like, says Roswitha and rummages in the sideboard for the keys. Perhaps I'll come up once and check on you? asks Roswitha.

You? No. But send Bruno up to me, says Martha.

Bruno? Is Bruno supposed to come here? Did he say so?

Martha makes a hand gesture toward the sewing room and answers with a hard voice: Bruno will come, you can rely on that. Don't forget! Send him up to me. Farewell.

Roswitha gives Martha one key for the iron door to the attic and one for the small room and is relieved that Martha isn't staying after all, because the window seats, the box seats, are really more than taken. She also thinks that she can't stand another person in her apartment. She will have to flee from the disturbance, Roswitha is already thinking, if it goes on like this for days. Besides, more workdays will be lost if the people on the roof don't reach an agreement soon.

When Roswitha returns, Max and his friends have red faces and the obstinate watery gaze of drunks. Fred thinks they will soon have to get a fresh supply because the beer is already running out. Roswitha wants to object, she is getting worried. But Lotte is thirsty too, and Greta giggles that she is too. The crowd in the garden still hasn't dispersed; on the contrary, more and more people are coming. Only a few are leaving. What's new is that some are setting up folding chairs and tables, bringing out bread and thermoses or beer bottles and starting to have a snack. They are talking more and more loudly, waving their arms excitedly, cursing the men on the roof and wanting to shoot them down like sparrows.

Roswitha feels a violent dislike of the crowd of people in the garden, indeed of all the people who are encroaching on her, leaving her almost no air to breathe and no room to do her work. But she doesn't dare to express her opinion and calms herself with the observation that it is a state of emergency that soon must end. And indeed, a scream goes through the crowd, even Max, who has the field glasses to his eyes again, roars; because the convicts have stood up and gone to the skylight. They seem to want to climb the roof with the help of the rope ladder to go back inside. The civilian, who really is a psychiatrist, as Lotte suspected, is already stretching out his arms through the opening toward the men; but then the two pause in their climb, shake their heads and creep back again to their place behind the snow guard. The people in the audience, who feel that they've been made fools of, howl with outrage. Those who have stood up from the grass sit down again, and those who have managed to get a comfortable place on the Caterpillar take their place again. These are mainly young people, who are also climbing around on the steam shovel.

Roswitha is no longer in the mood to stand behind Max or the others and stare at the church roof and the two figures of misery; and she wishes someone would come who would rescue her from this situation, would simply lead her away and talk with her about entirely ordinary things or about the planned performance of the historical tragedy. She thinks of the school inspector again, of his courtesy and his sensitivity. Inconceivable that he would derive such pleasure from this whole business. She deliberates whether she should climb up to Martha in the attic, even though she told her not to, but dismisses the idea again because she doesn't want to risk getting into an argument with her sister. Furthermore, she would rather not leave Max alone with the others in her apartment.

If she could not have been certain that the escapees would have to leave the roof sometime in some manner or other, and that everyday life and the ordered course of events would be restored again, she would now be in despair. She is exhausted, so she retreats to the bedroom. But even there she cannot shake off her depression; when she looks at the beds, she remembers what has happened in them, and it seems to her as if there is no place for her any more in the entire apartment. She sits at the window, looks at the river, then lays her head on her arms and begins to sob bitterly. She thinks she is going to suffocate, then she screams into the rushing of the water, heaves out a breath and moans, in this manner she becomes calmer and finally falls asleep huddled up at the window.

When someone touches her on the shoulder, Roswitha starts up. Night has fallen. Lotte has been looking for her because important visitors have arrived, as she says. Roswitha, who is still haunted by an alarming dream, wants to protest against further intruders. But Lotte interrupts her, her brother-in-law has come and the school inspector. Both are asking about her.

Roswitha runs her hands over her hair and smoothes her dress as she gets up quickly. The school inspector and Bruno actually have made themselves comfortable in front of the window. Fred and Kurti have lent them their places. Now they are sprawled on Roswitha's bed. The school inspector, whose face is flushed, confesses to her as he greets her, staggering slightly, that he has never experienced such a highly dramatic moment; this moment, or rather this spectacle, is for him, for his dramatic inspiration, of inestimable value, and he therefore hopes that she will excuse his unannounced entry into her apartment.

This speech sends Max into uncontrollable laughter. For quite some time he is unable to stop, and snorts his laughter out into the night. Bruno, who has seated himself beside Greta, says he has just come past for a minute. He has to go again right away.

Your wife is waiting for you in the attic. You are supposed to go up, says Roswitha, feeling shocked that she has forgotten her sister for such a long time.

What? asks Bruno, in the attic, here?

Yes, she has a better view there, says Roswitha uncertainly. The attic idea now seems to her a crazy idea of her sister's.

She's waiting for you.

She's waiting for me, says Bruno with a curious expression, and as he says so he looks the librarian in the eyes. Well, then I probably immediately have to ... It was a brief pleasure. Goodbye, he does up the zipper of his jacket, bows exaggeratedly to all sides and goes. Soon afterwards Miss Greta leaves too. Roswitha breathes a sigh of relief. Now there is room at the window again; and Martha would probably also go home with Bruno.

Lotte is sitting between Max and the school inspector. For Roswitha there is still a place free on the other side of Hingerl. She moves up to the window now, beside the schoolteacher, who is turned toward Lotte. The two men are still crouching on the roof in the merciless island of light of the floodlights. Meanwhile it has gotten cool, and mosquitoes and moths hum around the lamp, but no one thinks of closing the window.

Without saying anything, Roswitha would like to know how long the uninvited guests are going to stay at her place. But she doesn't dare to ask out loud, especially not now that the school inspector himself has come. Suddenly her sister occurs to her again, and she calms herself with the thought that Bruno will have brought her down from the attic and taken her home. Nevertheless, a sudden feeling of apprehension sends her to the attic door. She presses the handle, the door is locked and there is no key in the lock. Roswitha thinks it over and then comes to the plausible conclusion that her sister and brother-in-law, probably in order not to bother her anymore and also not to be bothered themselves anymore, had silently gone home and absent-mindedly taken the key with them. Tomorrow or the next day they would certainly bring it back.

Roswitha hasn't been gone long, and yet the mood in the room has changed. Max, his head supported in both hands, is staring stupidly and drunkenly into the night. The inspector has taken Lotte's hand in his and is talking quietly to her. Unnoticed by him, Roswitha sits down beside Hingerl again. Fred and Kurti are snoring on Roswitha's bed. Roswitha hears Lotte's whispered confession to the school inspector that she can finally look up to her husband, Hermann, again, because he obviously comes shining through in such a dangerous and important matter. She admires how he takes action, the school inspector, whom she calls Alfonse, must admit that he does too. She is almost sobbing while the man she is talking to is stroking her hand and arm and whispering back: Of course. Of course. Finally Lotte lays her head on the shoulder of the man who is stroking her, causing her artistically arranged red hair to become disarrayed and a heavy strand separates itself out from the tower of hair and falls in waves over the inspector's back. Max has fallen asleep on the table, and Alfonse Xavier Hingerl is kissing Lotte's closed eyes. It is very quiet and cozy in the room. The sleepers on Roswitha's bed are no longer snoring. The yellow light of the table lamp creates a romantic light. Over on the church roof the two men now attempt to crawl out of the gleaming spotlight, but it catches up to them again almost as soon as they come to its edge and keeps them in the middle of the beam. Finally they give up and stretch out behind the snow guard. Roswitha stays on her chair as if she is under a spell and pulls her opera glass out of her apron pocket. She tries to find the young man again in her field of vision. The two fellows have put their jackets back on again and have moved very close together, probably to keep each other warm. All the same, Roswitha can clearly see through her glass that Pius's shoulders are shivering from the cold. He has covered his face with his hands. Maybe he is crying and is shaken by his sobbing, Roswitha wonders, and the thought moves her deeply. The old man has put his arm around the young one and is staring straight ahead; Roswitha has the feeling, and it makes her uneasy, that he is looking into her eyes or right through her. Suddenly he moves, gives his partner a nudge, the boy takes his hands away from his face – the opera glass is too weak for her to be able to determine without a doubt whether there are traces of tears on his face, in any case the two of them are now looking spellbound over to her, as Roswitha now firmly believes. All at once the two of them act excited. They stretch out their arms and point at her, wave their arms around, turn their heads, as if they wanted to make themselves noticed, Roswitha also recognizes by the movements of their mouths that they are probably calling. But no one hears them. And they still have their eyes directed at her. What is there to see about her? What is behind her? Beside her? That's just all crazy, she says to herself, they probably can't even make me out at this distance, at most the light in the window and the people in it perhaps as shadows. They are moving, Roswitha tells herself, to keep themselves warm. Finally they give up and stretch out behind the snow guard. Well there you have it, thinks Roswitha, they did give me a fright. She ought to stand up and go away and send the strangers out of her apartment. But confused as she is, she can't rouse herself to do anything.

Lotte opens her eyes again and swats at a mosquito. She says quietly to Alfonse that Hermann will have to be present on the crisis committee all night tonight. Roswitha hears everything and also sees that the inspector, on hearing that, raises Lotte's hand to his lips. Then the two of them stand up, and only then do they discover Roswitha on her chair because Hingerl has banged into it. Roswitha is astonished at how well they cover up their embarrassment. Unfortunately they will have to go, perhaps they will come back tomorrow if the two fools haven't given up in the meantime or fallen down. The school inspector stands at attention when he is saying goodbye to Roswitha. She can still hear him say as he is leaving that a democracy that is unavoidably lacking a strong man does have its faults. Such incidents, and he turns once again to Roswitha, would not have happened in his time. You understand? Not everything was bad in his time. Roswitha, who has never concerned herself with *his time* – she was still a child in *his time* – nods anyway and answers that she has never heard otherwise. A clever woman, Alfonse Hingerl is pleased. Then Roswitha brings the two to the door, where Lotte secretly squeezes her hand and whispers in her ear: It was very nice at your place.

Suddenly all has become very quiet around her. All the people have left the parish garden too. Even in her workshop, where Max and his friends are sleeping off their intoxication, quiet has returned. She is afraid that her return might disturb this peace that she so urgently needs after this day. She is counting on the last uninvited visitors to disappear of their own accord sometime in the night. The fact that the school inspector also came to watch the escapees from her window disappointed her on the one hand – she thought him too fine and educated to join the common people in gloating over the misery of these wretched figures – on the other hand his appearance did please her for a short while. On the whole though, his behavior has tarnished her memory of him and his kiss on her hand.

Roswitha is already falling asleep when she is startled by a banging sound that must come from something falling over or falling down. After that though, everything is quiet, so she soon falls asleep again.

On this night, Max doesn't even get out of his clothes. He throws himself on the bed beside her in his shirt and pants and is still lying there the next morning as if he never wants to wake up again. She observes him with loathing. Just don't wake him. In the workshop, his buddies are starting to move. Roswitha stamps her foot when she sees the two of them: They are still there! In the meantime, they rub their eyes, click their tongues and open their drowsy mouths up wide.

Roswitha grumpily begins to collect the empty bottles and glasses in her workshop and to put the chairs back in place, while the two sit around with dull eyes or relieve themselves in the lavatory. On the church roof, one of the convicts, the old one, has sat up and claps his arms crosswise against his upper body. He is probably freezing, because the nights are already autumnal, cold and damp. The other one is still lying motionless like a dark beam. In the skylight there is no one to be seen. The clock is just now striking eight. The parish garden is abandoned, except for the prison guards, the police and the ambulance. It seems the escapees have already become old news, incapable of drawing anyone out – at least not at such an early hour. Roswitha thinks about what she should do next. The shopping is probably the most important thing. And all the sewing work that is overdue! Of course she can't begin to think about that as long as her workshop is besieged by the uninvited guests. She tries to estimate how long the two men can still stand to be up on the roof. She is astonished at their stubbornness. It must be dreadfully uncomfortable up there in the long run. Besides, it is boiling hot during the day, so that the roof tiles heat up, and at night there is the cold. They are exposed to that without protection.

There is still no workman to be seen on the scaffolding around her house. As if they all knew that the exceptional situation was still continuing.

Something moves behind Roswitha's back. Short, quick Kurti Schweinschwaller taps her on the shoulder: Scuse me ma'am, where can we get washed at your place?

Roswitha flares up: I'm not a hotel!

Kurti laughs, smacks himself on the mouth: Pardon, but that was good. No, seriously. A little water, soap and a towel. It's urgently needed.

Why don't you go back where you come from and wash yourselves there? asks Roswitha sharply and is convinced that she has finally found the right tone.

But look, then Max would be angry with us if we took off without so much as adieu, Kurti explains patiently. Alfred is grinning behind him. You don't want to do that, do you, make him angry? Or? No, my dear ma'am, as far as washing is concerned, anything is good enough for us.

Then she gives up. She shows them the washbasin and other things in the kitchen. In order not to have to look at the two of them as they are getting washed, she grabs her shopping basket and goes to do the shopping.

The whole village is out and about. Leokadia Braml's grocery store is bursting full. That means waiting. The women, it is almost exclusively women, discuss the two gangsters' exciting escape attempt. Roswitha doesn't hear anything new. When it is finally her turn, she is already quite exhausted from standing, but she still has to go to the baker's. There too the customers are jammed into the narrow salesroom; she has never experienced it like that. The stores otherwise get only a handful of customers so early in the morning.

On the way home she moves along with her full shopping basket almost as if in a procession. Everyone is rushing to the vicinity of the escapees. Roswitha is pushed, jostled and swept along. The limping woman is in the way of those who are pressing straight ahead. Finally she arrives at her own house. The stream of people washes her up in front of the door like flotsam. She is relieved she has managed it and pulls herself with her shopping basket up the stairs.

In her apartment there is already plenty going on. She foresaw and feared it. They have brought in beer again and liquor too. Max has climbed out of bed; he is sitting in the sewing room with Kurti and Alfred at the table; for breakfast he has already drunk a beer.

The parish garden fills up with people; the rope ladder is hanging out the skylight again as an offer to the convicts. The skylight itself, however, is still unoccupied. And in Roswitha's workshop the uninvited men are wildly and willfully wrecking havoc. Max is throwing knives again. The others watch and stamp their feet and clap when he hits the middle of the circles drawn on the board. At the same time they keep an eye on what is happening outside, because something has to happen there soon, everyone thinks, it's in the air.

Roswitha stands silently in the room a short while and doesn't know how she should behave. No one is aware that she is there. One of the fine knives like a stiletto is lying on the floor a little off to one side and next to it her long scissors for cutting heavy materials. Max has obviously also tried to hit the target with this implement. Roswitha bends down quickly and puts the big scissors in her apron pocket, though the top half of them is protruding. She intends to bring this important tailor's utensil into safety from the men.

Until now neither Lotte nor the school inspector has come, nor Miss Greta. Roswitha hides herself away in the bedroom and sits at the window there to stare at the river. When she has looked a long while into the swirling water and at the fields and woods, she feels miserable, because the view of the quiet landscape devoid of people has nothing to do with the events in the other part of her apartment, nothing at all to do with life. The meadows, the trees and the fields know about nothing and are also unable to comfort her, even if they are so lovely to behold, they cannot give her advice. It is also not possible to disappear in the landscape, to find her place in nature. Even from the most beautiful nature there always has to be a way back to people again, at least to the house, under a roof, and that means, of course, to the people who would never let her be by herself again as she was before, she feels that indistinctly, but full of melancholy. Max has broken into her life, has beaten a broad path into her everyday life and lets everyone, everyone in. She finds it unsettling that she doesn't know whether she wants to have everything exactly as it was before and live all alone. After all, Max has become close to her, closer than anyone else has ever been, and for the most part it has been terrible, but now and then it has also been good, or it is such that she thinks maybe something good could still come of it, although her heart gets heavy at the thought of the devastation that his being here has brought.

Where is her brother-in-law? She expected him or her sister back again for sure before noon with the keys to the attic.

Suddenly she is so concerned about the locked door to the attic that she feels compelled to go there, and when she is standing in front of it she presses on the handle and rattles at the door as if she is out of her senses. That's foolish. So she runs back into the apartment, because it isn't clear to her what she is doing here; there is a second key to the attic that she must be able to find somewhere. In her search for it she flits through the apartment, tears drawers open, rummages through them. In her sewing room she is seized again by helpless rage against Max and his knife throwing, while the audience in the parish garden gets loudly excited about the escapees, those outlaws beyond their reach. The spectators standing closely packed in the enclosure call out to the custodians of the law: How long do you want to put up with that? The atmosphere is strained to the limit when Roswitha comes to the window. The people feel that the persistence of the escapees has made fools of them personally; these gangsters have led them around by the nose. There is no getting at them from below and they will have to be got down if law and order still prevail here. And it's easy to see what happens when they get their way; no decent citizen is safe any more from these criminals, about whom so much fuss is made; and it turns out – one of the onlookers who has particularly sharp binoculars spreads the news – that the rascals are getting roast pork with dumplings today, probably served with bread dumplings and sauerkraut. And one of the criminals has crapped in the eaves trough; we're letting these scoundrels shit on our heads, that's how far things have gone.

Roswitha is excited by this seething unrest that rises up to her so-called box seat at the window, it vaguely frightens her and distracts her from her search for the key. And she sits down at the table, where there is room now because all three men are throwing knives, although they are no longer hitting the mark, they are just throwing wildly against the wall, against the wooden door, and it's lucky they didn't hit Roswitha, who came in through that very door. Lotte waves up to her from below. She and the school inspector and the librarian are trying to climb up a caterpillar shovel. When they don't succeed in this, the three decide to come to Roswitha again. But they remain standing in the doorway and shake their heads when they see the men throwing knives. The school inspector sighs: We don't want to interrupt. And Lotte looks reproachfully at Roswitha. Miss Greta says cheerfully that she knows where there is a pile of wood or logs from where they can have a good view and that is easy to climb and not yet known about. Off to the lookout, calls the inspector happily and does a sharp about-turn. Lotte turns to Roswitha again and shakes her head, and again there is reproach in her friend's look, as if she, Roswitha, had arranged for the knife throwing. She does hold up her hands as a sign of her helplessness, but Lotte doesn't see them or pay attention to them any more. Then Roswitha remembers the attic door and she tears open several drawers in the little cabinet in the hall and rummages around in them. And in fact, between the string, cork bottle stoppers, scissors and other odds and ends, it turns up. Well there it is! she exclaims in relief. I'll go right up, she says with the key in her hand and stands in front of the iron attic door and doesn't go up, but stands there and waits and says: Now I'm going to go up, and doesn't go up, but rather to the window of the hall, and sees how curious people are still pushing into the parish garden that is already crammed quite full with people, but Bruno is not among them, and neither is Martha.

Then she goes to the attic door and opens it and tells herself that in a minute she'll have to laugh with relief, because relief and reassurance are certainly lying in wait for her in the attic, not their opposite. So she opens the door, climbs up the stone steps and goes up higher and higher on them. The house has a huge loft, like old Black Forest houses that sometimes seem to consist only of roofs. And she starts to hum a tune to herself, and when she pays attention to which tune has come to mind, she stands still and is annoyed, because it is the song that the accordion player played incessantly a few days ago and that kept her from getting to sleep, and he had bawled out the words to it, and now she can't get them out of her head either: In a Polish town, hum, hum, she was the most beautiful child in all of Poland, but no, but no, she said, I will never kiss. In a Polish pond, they found a corpse, so pale ... a shameful song. She wants to forget it. She goes farther and reaches the end of the stone stairs. Now she has an overview of the entire attic, if she looks around. She looks around and doesn't notice that she is starting to hum again. The attic is also a drying loft. And look, someone has taken down her washing and folded it neatly in the basket. Admittedly, the clothesline has been taken down too. It is gone. Laundry there, line gone. And otherwise? There is no one there. Then she calls out in high spirits: Martha, where are you? Such nonsense, she is of course at home with her husband Bruno. Sleeping in or doing something else that is sensible. Maybe she really has to go into hospital. Maybe she told Bruno and he is with her so she won't be afraid. Martha, Martha! she calls happily. She could have jumped with relief. But she goes to her compartment in the attic, behind an enclosure that still lets her have a good view of everything from outside: No one. The skylight is open. Martha must have looked through it for a while at the activity on the church roof across the way, because there is a stool under the skylight, actually it's their mother's former washstand with the warped plywood top.

The compartment is not locked. Everything empty. Everything empty. Her sister long since at home. Her foot bumps into a stool that is lying tipped over beside the washstand. She can turn back again. But then she does climb up on the washstand and stretch her head out the attic window. And there is the window hook and tied to the window hook is the line, the rope, the clothesline, and on this line – the roof drops steeply – something is hanging, something is tied to it, something with a head and hair on its head, and it is a person, it is Martha. And hangs and lies on the roof on the rope that is pulled very tight, and she can't see the face, just the hair, the part. The gray hair that has grown out under the dyed brown hair. This part looks like someone else's, but it is her sister, she recognizes the dress and the shoes and her hands and her arms that are lying completely still next to her body, and her face is not to be seen because it is lying on the roof, directly against the roof tiles, and she is out of reach. Roswitha doesn't understand anything, why outside there, why on her roof, and she starts to hum the shameful song again and pulls the big sharp tailor's scissors, that she is fortunately still carrying around with her, out of her skirt, and cuts and cuts, cuts the rope, cuts through the clothesline, and Martha slowly begins to move and slides down, down, goes faster, turns around, her dress rides up over her hips, her arms spread out, the figure drifts toward the snow guard and comes to rest on it.

Roswitha drones: There I found a corpse, she held the note in her hand ... and runs down the stairs and hums, in which was written ... Then Bruno is actually standing in front of her and seems out of breath, he is puffing, he is worked up, and he doesn't fail to ask the question, in the midst of her humming: Is my wife here with you?

Then Roswitha pauses and says: But of course, certainly, indeed at my place. I've already told you that. Said so yesterday. She's still waiting for you. Up in the attic. Go on up, she's waiting.

Then she runs into the workshop. And in the workshop things are pretty wild. They are throwing the knives and drinking and shouting, and Roswitha says to Max out of her humming:

And now I want this to stop. Stop. Stop. Stop.

Then Max starts to laugh terribly, so she can see past his rotten teeth deep down his throat, and the others are laughing too and holding their stomachs for laughter. And Max comes toward Roswitha and says:

So. So. Stop, and stamps his feet in time, so. Stop, she says. Stop. And stamps. And brays with laughter. And Roswitha goes toward him and says: Stop. Stop. Stop.

So, why stop. Why then, why then, says Max and wants to grab her by the arms and push her around in jest: Why stop. So. So. Stop. Why.

But she doesn't let herself be caught, reaches instead into her apron pocket, and when he spreads out his arms again and wants to grab her, then she plunges in the scissors from her apron pocket. And plunges them in. And since he raises his arms once more as if he wanted to catch her again, she plunges them in once more, further down, with all her strength, and then he doubles up and puts his hands on his stomach and clenches himself more and more tightly and falls over. That makes a clatter. But very quietly and suddenly the other two dart away.

A yell comes up from the parish garden, such as is sometimes heard from football fields. Roswitha sits down at the table and looks at the church roof. There the two men are in the process of climbing up the rope ladder and going in through the skylight.

Afterword[3]

One would not deduce from reading *Winter Quarters* that Evelyn Grill is happily married: and indeed, there was a time in her life when, like the main character, she was struggling to strike a balance between self-realization and married life. The theme is perennial. Those left too long on their own suffer from loneliness, while those who have too little time to themselves feel overwhelmed by the demands of others. Most of Grill's works to date are memorable portrayals of the problematic attractions and drawbacks of intimate relationships.

With her first short story, "Fluchtbewegungen," 1982 (Escapist Activities), Evelyn Grill established herself as a writer who tells a good story with vivid imagery and an underlying sense of ironic humor. Daunted by the never-ending household chores and demands of her family, a trapped housewife finds a creative release in decorative glass painting, only to have that activity deemed a sign of mental illness. Grill describes a similar situation in her first novel, *Rahmenhandlungen*, 1985 (Sub-Plots), written from the perspective of a woman preparing to free herself from a critical and controlling husband. He is seeking to improve their sexual relations, while she is more interested in intellectual pursuits. The title is one of the plays on words that Grill so enjoys: in the attempt to keep his wife in her place, the husband sets limits (*Rahmen*) to her actions (*Handlungen*), reducing their significance to sub-plots (*Rahmenhandlungen*). Grill admits that much of the material in the novel is autobiographical.

Whereas the female protagonists of these first two works feel the need to retreat from their families in order to get in touch with their inner selves again, Grill's next two works deal with the opposite problem. They portray independent women who are so lonely that their choice of companions is indiscriminate. Problems

---

[3] I am grateful to Evelyn Grill for promptly answering all my questions about her work.

with the companions then get the women in trouble with the law. Grill wrote *Winterquartier*, 1993 (*Winter Quarters*, 2004) in response to a sensational murder in Austria.[4] She felt the woman was condemned by the press before coming to trial. In the novel, Grill creates a situation so complex that no clear-cut verdict is possible. She has shifted the emphasis from what happened to why it happened. With the best of intentions, Roswitha Mantler, a single, forty-two year-old tailor, takes in Max Leimer, one of the masons working on the outside of her apartment building, and ends up killing him. In Grill's next book, *Wilma*, 1994, she again sets circumstances and personal interests on a collision course, with the tragedy this time being death through criminal negligence. After the ungainly and mentally retarded Wilma is abandoned by her mother, she is taken in by Agnes, a lonely widow who lavishes attention on her. Wilma becomes the focal point of Agnes's life, but the girl is raped and becomes pregnant. When Wilma needs medical attention while giving birth, Agnes is so afraid the authorities will take the girl away from her that she fails to act in time. Both *Winter Quarters* and *Wilma* portray lonely women who take in someone most people would consider undesirable, and their emotional involvement with that person brings about their downfall. Bizarre though these situations are, Grill uses them to call into question what we usually consider to be normal behavior, to unmask the motives of respected members of society, and to show the brutality of crowds.

Her next book, *Hinüber*, 1999 (Passing Away), again has autobiographical elements. The Austrian town to which the main character returns is clearly Garsten, Grill's birthplace in Upper Austria. She portrays the deeply concerned, but superficially hypocritical behavior of family members as a young man is dying of cancer; their hypocrisy is dictated in part by the physician's deceptive approach to his terminally ill patient. Prepared words of deep meaning remain unsaid, tears are shed in secret, and after a

---

[4] In the spring of 1974, Anne Madler ended twenty years of beatings and sexual abuse by killing her husband in his sleep with a heavy mason's hammer and then disposing of his body in the woods near St. Polten, Austria. The crime writer Max Haines published his account of the murder in the *Toronto Sun* newspaper on Saturday, January 8, 1989.

short stay the main character returns to her life in Germany. The excruciating inadequacy of interpersonal relationships shown in *Hinüber* stands in sharp contrast to the hilarious monologues of self-analysis in Grill's effervescent story *Ins Ohr*, 2002 (*On the Phone*, 2004). The speaker is surprised by her husband's decision to leave her just as she is completing her training as a lawyer. She then becomes involved with other men, discovering in the process why they are available. Unlike Roswitha in *Winter Quarters*, who repeatedly tries to put the best possible constructions on outrageous actions, Grill's main characters in *Hinüber* and *Ins Ohr* are quick to deconstruct illusions. Their realism is respectively sobering and entertaining.

Grill's thought-provoking subject matter, her dramatic plots, straightforward style and tonal diversity make her works unforgettable. After writing the humorous *Ins Ohr*, she turned again to darker material. The novel *Vanitas oder Hofstätters Begierden*, 2004 (*Vanitas* or Hofstätter's Passions) examines the falseness of an affluent couple who have lost all respect for each other but still strive to keep up the appearance of being happily married. Again, Grill exposes the stressful emotions of a marriage gone sour.

Born Evelyn Holzapfel on January 15, 1942 in Garsten, Upper Austria, Grill has early childhood memories of World War II. Although the small town of Garsten suffered no direct damage, she remembers having to spend nights in the cellar with her mother, and emerging in the mornings to see contrails from planes that had bombed nearby Steyr and Linz. The family was adequately supplied with essential food from her maternal grandparents' farm, but the children missed sweets and appreciated the chocolate they sometimes received from American soldiers.

Grill's father died of kidney failure when she was ten years old. He was a Social Democrat who refused to join the Nazi (National Socialist German Workers') Party, even when called upon to do so. However, he was not a member of the resistance. As an engineer on a train he provided an essential service, so he was not drafted. Grill's mother later told her that he suffered terribly from what he witnessed, because for a while he drove trains with far too many people penned into the cars. Grill explores the mindset of a locomotive driver in her short story "Endstation," 1985 (End of the Line).

Grill had a younger brother who was also the engineer on a train. Her older sister is a tailor. Their family name, Holzapfel, means crab-apple in German, and Grill concedes that one of the reasons for her early marriage was to change her surname. She married Johann Grill when she was nineteen and had two daughters and a son with him. Evidently content with the surname Grill, which has the same meaning in German as in English, she has retained it as her pen name, although she has been happily married since 1986 to the respected Germanist Joachim W. Storck.

She was pleased to discover in school that the Austrian poet and dramatist Franz Grillparzer (1791-1872), whose writing she greatly admires, was also born on January 15. Grill began to write during her first marriage, much as her main character in "Fluchtversuche" began decorative glass painting. Her husband regarded her writing with skepticism and disapproval. However, the well-established author Gertrud Fussenegger (1912-), who lives in Leonding near Linz, recognized Grill's talent and encouraged her to become a writer.

While still living in Austria, Grill also began to study law in Linz, but did not finish the degree because her marriage to Storck took her to the town of Marbach am Neckar in Germany, where he worked in the German Literary Archive. Grill's contribution to the *Festschrift* celebrating his 75th birthday is a witty short story, "Besuch bei der Augenzeugin," 1998 (Visiting the Eyewitness), depicting the delicate negotiations involved in obtaining material for the Archive. Following Storck's retirement, they moved in 1992 to Freiburg im Breisgau, where Grill attends classes in art history at the university.

Grill's writing has been promoted both by Austria and by Germany. She began publishing shorter works in magazines and newspapers in 1980 and received a prize from the Austrian city of Steyr in 1982 (the *Steyrer Literaturförderungspreis*), the year in which her story "Fluchtbewegungen" (Escapist Activities) was included in the anthology *Arbeite, Frau ...* (Work, Woman ...) published by the Wiener Frauenverlag (the Viennese Women's Publishing Company). In 1983/84 she achieved national recognition when she was awarded a Scholarship for Literature from the Austrian Federal Ministry of Education, Art, and Sport. The same Ministry awarded her a book prize for *Rahmenhandlungen* (Sub-Plots) in 1985, and other awards and honors followed in rapid succession. Grill has received scholarships and financial assistance from the German province of Baden-Württemberg in 1995, 1997, 2000 and 2002. Meanwhile, the Austrian government has continued to recognize her with Rome Scholarships in 1999 and 2002, and with financial assistance and scholarships from the Austrian Department for the Arts in 2000 and 2003.

Winter Quarters is unmistakably set in Garsten, Grill's birthplace, and was first published in hard cover with sixteen uncaptioned photographs[5] of the area. In the context of the novel, some features of the place acquire heightened significance. Roswitha's upstairs apartment has windows on three sides. It looks out on a church with onion towers, a church that is unusual because one wing of it has been turned into a prison. The Garsten Parish website (*Pfarre Garsten*) has pictures of both the outside and inside of the beautiful Baroque church, and confirms that a wing of it has been used as a prison since 1850. Grill reports that prisoners did break out onto the roof, and the crowd's reaction was as she describes it. Placed in the context of the novel, though, that episode resonates with Roswitha's reflections on freedom, reflections that become ironic when one considers that she herself will likely spend time in custody. The constant rushing sound of the river provides the backdrop to Roswitha's thoughts, and seems to remind her that time is passing. She is getting older, and is not yet married. The river Enns, in which Evelyn Holzapfel almost drowned when she was seven years old, has since been rerouted.[6] And finally, Roswitha's apartment looks out on the street, where she can see as far as an elderberry bush. Those who leave her apartment disappear from view when they pass the elderberry bush, sometimes forever.

---

[5] Grill, Evelyn. *Winterquartier*. Weitra, Austria: *publication PN°1*, Bibliothek der Provinz, 1993. Photos by Gerald Kapfer, St. Ulrich bei Steyr.

[6] In an interview published in the *Steyrer Rundschau* newspaper on May 8, 2003, Grill belatedly thanks the man who saved her life by pulling her from the river.

Her parents' accidental deaths when she was fourteen have made her acutely aware of the possibility of abandonment and cause her to overreact to Max's failure to appear when expected.

The outside of the apartment building serves as both setting and metaphor. It is increasingly defaced by masons chipping off the plaster until it and the grounds around it are in a state of devastation. Garsten is preparing for its 1000-year jubilee and old buildings must be renovated, but the novel does not follow the work past the wrecking stage. The effect the masons are having on the outside of the building is closely paralleled by the effect Max and his friends have on Roswitha's orderly life. They figuratively chip away at her, disrupting her work schedule and making a mess of her apartment. She attempts to make herself more attractive by getting an expensive new hairdo, but this is futile. These men are going to drag her down. The destructive work on the exterior of the apartment is mirrored by the effects of Max's knife-throwing hobby on the inside. Again, the effect is both literal and figurative. He finds it hilarious that the picture in the master bedroom is of the heart of Mary pierced with seven swords. Yet by taking advantage of Roswitha sexually without the slightest consideration for her personally, by moving in with her with no long-term sense of commitment, he is piercing her heart as well. Any semblance of initial courtesy quickly disappears, and the drunken knife-throwers use Roswitha's tailor's dummy with the woman's dirndl on it as their target. They are narrowing in on Roswitha herself.

Grill uses several techniques to help make understandable Roswitha's tolerance of the escalating violence. One of these is the subtle use of literary references. In contrast to the Austrian author Elfriede Jelinek (1946-), who writes works rich in intertextuality that address problems in the Austrian way of thinking, Grill seeks to make her references understandable to a readership not necessarily steeped in Austrian or even European culture. For example, her short story "Rosen-Zeit," 1986 (Roses Time) is clearly critical of the slow-paced lifestyle portrayed in Adalbert Stifter's famous novel, *Der Nachsommer*, 1857 (*Indian Summer*, 1985), but the story also makes perfect sense if the reader does not recognize the reference. Likewise, the unnamed German poet repeatedly referred to in Grill's *Hinüber* is Rainer Maria Rilke, so well known to educated Germans that the name is redundant, but so well integrated into the events in Grill's book that no further knowledge of him is necessary. The references to German literature in *Winter Quarters* are from *Grimms' Fairy Tales*, and help define Roswitha's wishful way of thinking. Before she and Max sleep together, she thinks of the bed as the "nuptial" bed, taking the word from a fairytale. After they sleep together, she dutifully and contentedly tidies the room, thinking of herself as the industrious girl in "Mother Holle," the girl who is rewarded with gold coins. Likewise, on her way home after the first meeting with the cast of the historical pageant, Roswitha feels as if a horn of plenty were pouring out its contents over her head, thereby identifying herself with the female figure in the fairytale "The Star Coins" who was rewarded because she was so good to others. So she persists in trying to turn Max into a respectable husband, long after it is evident to the reader that he is a frog, not a prince.

Yet Grill shows by comparison with other male-female relationships portrayed in the novel that the problem with Max's behavior is simply one of degree. None of the men is perfect. Roswitha's father regularly brought home his friends from work for an evening of drinking, smoking and playing cards, leaving her mother to clean up the mess the following day. They stopped short of smashing things, but so did Max the first time he had his friends over. By cleaning up after them, Roswitha is just falling into the servile female role she observed in her own mother. Her sister Martha does the same thing. Following her diagnosis of breast cancer she needs moral support, but does not receive it. Yet she keeps that to herself, and serves tea to her husband when he complains of a slight stomach ache, even though she knows he is betraying her by having an affair with a single woman. In the course of the novel, Grill also tarnishes the reputation of the initially respected school inspector, the distinguished gentleman who kisses Roswitha's hand. He flirts with her married friend Lotte at Roswitha's apartment, and when it becomes apparent that Lotte's husband, the prison guard, will be on duty throughout the night, the inspector and Lotte leave together. He takes what he can get.

As does Max, who says quite honestly that he is looking for winter quarters.

Grill gives Max just enough positive qualities to prolong Roswitha's indecision. He has rotten teeth, but is physically strong and well-built and more attractive than Lotte's husband. Given that Roswitha walks with a pronounced limp from childhood polio, she feels very fortunate to have found a good-looking partner. Max is also refreshingly direct, and greets the inspector's pretentious speech with a loud burst of laughter. Armin Ayren's review of *Winterquartier* in the *Badische Zeitung*, 1993, astutely points out that there is no guilty party in the novel, there are only victims.[7] Although Roswitha dreams from the start of marriage, a close reading of the text reveals that as a misunderstanding. What Max Leimer actually says is that he is looking for a woman. The word he uses, *Frau*, can also mean wife in German, but neither Max's words nor his actions indicate any expectation on his part that the cohabitation will be long-lasting. He is not dishonest, or even intentionally misleading.

Max and Roswitha are both handicapped by their learned behavior patterns, and their union makes for a volatile situation. Max has obviously gotten through life by moving in on single women and taking advantage of them until they throw him out. The one before Roswitha got rid of him by reporting him to the police for something, and the resulting criminal record cost him his job with the railway. But he has no way of knowing that Roswitha will go so far as to kill him. She, in turn, is sending mixed signals. Angry speeches are followed by rationalized reconciliations. While realizing on the one hand that she has made a mistake in taking him in, she is on the other hand sexually fulfilled at last and unprepared to do without him. On the last morning in the novel, she hides in the bedroom and sits at the window there to stare at the river. The prison break-out across the way has kept Max and his friends in her apartment far longer than they would otherwise have been there. She is exhausted and upset by their drinking and misuse of her

---

[7] "Ein starkes Debüt: Evelyn Grills Roman 'Winterquartier.'" Badische Zeitung. Freiburg i. Br. 48. Jahrgang, Nr. 252, Samstag, 30. Oktober 1993 MAGAZIN Bücher, S.4.

sewing implements. If *Winter Quarters* were a drama, this would be her last soliloquy. She looks out at the lovely landscape devoid of people, at the river, fields, and willow trees, and realizes that it is "not possible to disappear in the landscape, to find her place in nature. Even from the most beautiful nature there always has to be a way back to people again."

Grill has a remarkable ability to create truly tragic situations. The dramatic ending of *Winter Quarters* cannot be attributed to a single factor, but rather to the convergence of several extremely stressful events. The commotion caused by the prison breakout is exacerbated by Max's drunken partying and knife-throwing, and the breaking point for Roswitha is her sister Martha's suicide in the loft. She could likely have dealt with any one of these events in isolation, but their combination overwhelms her. Everything is new to her. Roswitha and Max have not had enough time together either for her to decide calmly that he must go, or for them to work out their differences. In the end, it is a lack of communication that brings about his death. Roswitha does not bother trying to talk to him in his drunken state, and he mocks her, not knowing that she has just discovered her sister dead upstairs.

Arnold Stadler's discussion of the novel for *Deutsche Welle*, broadcast in February 1994, goes beyond the specifics of plot to capture the essence of Grill's accomplishment: "A thrilling book that holds our interest not by means of a foreground story, but by the intensity of its realization in writing. The urgent forward motion, the narrative orientation toward a catastrophe that we suspect, that is mirrored in the prisoners' revolt on the roof across the way, is expressed in language with a relentless rhythm suitable to the subject matter."[8]

One might also add that Grill seems to have worked with archetypal imagery. The English-speaking reader will be struck by the thematic similarities between Grill's *Winter Quarters* and Alfred Lord Tennyson's famous poem "The Lady of Shalott," written in 1832.[9] Both works deal with awakening sexuality that has disastrous

---

[8] Translated from Stadler's manuscript.
[9] *The English Parnassus: An Anthology Chiefly of Longer Poems.* Oxford: Clarendon Press, 1961. pp. 528-531.

consequences for the female protagonists. Both works are set in the autumn, by a river. Both women are extremely lonely and willing to make radical changes in their lives for the sake of the significant man who has come on the scene. And in both cases, it seems the man is not sufficiently aware of what the woman has done for him. There is a lack of verbal communication, and the woman acts in accordance with preconceived ideas from a background the man does not share or even understand. Both women spend their days sewing or weaving – until the man appears. And both women sing at the last.

The fairy Lady of Shalott sees the world only through a mirror, and is "half sick of shadows" by the time Sir Lancelot comes riding by. Although she knows that a curse will come upon her if she attempts to enter the world by looking down to Camelot, she takes the step in that direction, and immediately understands that she has gone the way of no return. The mirror cracks from side to side. Dying, she writes her name around the prow of a boat and floats downriver to her destination. Those who find her body are puzzled: "Who is this? and what is here?"

Likewise, Roswitha in *Winter Quarters* works hard to welcome the man everyone had assumed would never enter her life. She opens the master bedroom that has remained unused for decades, but the fairytale turns into a nightmare as she puts up with escalating vandalism and violence. By the time she admits to herself that she has made a mistake, a return to her former lifestyle seems both impossible and undesirable. Then her situation becomes intolerable, and those who find her humming to herself at the table will certainly be puzzled by the state of her apartment. In both cases, the question of whether to continue living alone or to make great sacrifices for the sake of having a mate has merged with the ultimate question of life or death.

Jean M. Snook